The Fifth Wall

Rachel Nagelberg

THE
FIFTH
WALL

A novel

Black Sparrow Books

David R. Godine, Publisher

BOSTON

This is
A Black Sparrow Book
Published in 2017 by
DAVID R. GODINE, PUBLISHER
Post Office Box 450
Jaffrey, New Hampshire 03452
www.blacksparrowbooks.com

LIBRARY OF CONGRESS CATALOGING-IN-PUBLICATION DATA
Names: Nagelberg, Rachel, author.
Title: The fifth wall : a novel / by Rachel Nagelberg.
Description: Jaffrey, New Hampshire : Black Sparrow Books, 2017.
Identifiers: LCCN 2016050041 | ISBN 9781574232288 (alk. paper)
Classification: LCC PS3614.A428 F54 2017 | DDC 813/.6—dc23
LC record available at https://lccn.loc.gov/2016050041

First edition, 2017
Printed in the United States of America

for my parents

The close-up in film treats the face primarily as a landscape; that is the definition of film, black hole and white wall, screen and camera. But the same goes for the earlier arts, architecture, painting, even the novel: close-ups animate and invent all of their correlations. So, is your mother a landscape or a face? A face or a factory?

GILLES DELEUZE AND FELIX GUATTARI,
A Thousand Plateaus

Love can tear anything to shreds.

KATHY ACKER,
Blood and Guts in High School

Prologue

I imagine the tumor as a dense, dark ball of mass, thick and strangled, icy black, pulsating. There is her forehead, covered with skin, a skin that coats the ivory bone of her skull, a skull that houses her gelatinous, salmon-pink brain tissue, a tissue that envelopes the black.

I've tried many times to visualize its origin—the split second when her body gave birth to terror—to the point where all my memories of her are now contaminated. The tumor is always there, existing invisibly, silently, waiting to attack.

First you prepare the site. You clear out your workspace, organize a plan. Out with the stone-trimmed gravel pathway, the three-tiered ceramic, solar-powered birdbath, the raised flowerbed you and your older brother, Caleb, helped her install. The budding fairy lilies, the anticipated thistle sage. Make sure to pull from beneath the roots, and then place carefully in the allotted pots and jars. The overgrown barberry bushes. The maidenhair ferns, the needlegrass. Say goodbye to the backyard, to the clover epidemic, the praying mantis mating ground, the labyrinth of cacti and succulents. The turtle sandbox that has growing inside it you-don't-even-wanna-know. The hanging stars and half-moons, the celestial copper sun. Take a good, long look. Capture it firmly in your mind.

There are memories that cannot be filmed.

Set up your demolition fencing, mark your roll-off locations. Organize your tools. Surround everything with yellow caution tape. From now on spaces will be called *areas*. Watch the walkways become *entry ramps*, the ground become a *zone*.

Out goes the interior garbage, the waste of human entropy, of past familial decay. Plastic containers, towering piles of paperbacks, magazines, and stacks of mail. Cardboard storage boxes bulging with old report cards, rubber-banded art projects, graded tests. Dust balls, loose change, long-lost erasers, pencils, pen caps, and pins. Then, of course, the furniture—the oak table, the polypropylene chairs, the mahogany breakfront, the bed frames, the end tables, bookcases, the dozen cat scratching posts, the torn-up leather lounge and loveseat. Into the Goodwill trucks they'll go—all these objects now lacking context, scattered and abandoned in indeterminate space.

I seriously considered complete demolition. The idea of using heavy, monstrous machines to attack and destroy satisfies me on a level I can't quite fully explain. The obvious reasons are of course for the spectacle of it, the energy, the violence—the immediate, crashing results. Why little boys like to set fire to inanimate objects and throw old TVs off the roof. Why we chuck things when we're angry. Why nuclear weapons exist. But the contractor, Jesse, suggested "deconstruction" as an alternative, *greener* way to go about it, which wouldn't make as much press—something I hadn't really thought about. There were the local Berkeley newspapers to consider, the affluent neighbors on the hills, and not to mention the restoration activists I'd almost definitely be fighting off. Plus Jesse was sexy, and I desperately wanted to please him. I've always been this way with men.

The camera wasn't intentional, at first. I'd set it up to capture a living moment of the house before it was destroyed, and then just left it on, mounted it more securely to the front lawn by burying the lower half of it like the stem of a beach umbrella into sand. It's now set up to record 24/7, transmitting the video to my MacBook like a surveillance camera, so that I can keep an eye on the site and monitor its progress, have the ability to see it live before me on a twelve-by-fifteen-inch screen.

Then go the fixtures, the appliances, all of the windows and doors. You separate the woods from the metals, the concretes, the disposables and the hazardous. The interior fixtures, the interior trim. Everything is placed in correctly marked areas, specified receptacles.

My art has always been about documentation. My unfinished thesis consists of me assembling entire rooms from my own fantasies, from my projected desires of a romantic future. I create three-dimensional settings filled with emptiness—spaces with no human presence, no narrative, no history. I film the process of each room from start to finish, which I then archive, and plan to display in exhibitions, where viewers will be invited into the makeshift rooms to experience the ghostly absence of a presence that never existed, sort of like walking into an apartment of someone who has just vanished into thin air. Spaces for the living dead.

I found her, I said for the record, and that was that.

They nodded with a practiced formality. I watched their pencils quiver.

For some reason I decided not to tell them—what I had witnessed, what I had seen.

I thought: how can you even identify someone without a face?

Let's rewind a little.

No one knew my mother was sick. It had been almost two years since I'd seen her—I'd been living across the country in Ithaca finishing up my MFA in Fine Art at Cornell. We rarely talked on the phone—the conversations always felt rushed and uneventful, lacking in drive or interest. My mother, a retired RN, lost from the years of her own increasing neuroses, with a ruthless addiction to television. She'd been living in that house alone for the past decade, having been divorced from my father for years—a professor of dramaturgy at Berkeley and ex-childhood actor. He'd been living on a sailboat docked in Marin for the past few years with a three-legged German Shepherd named Pozzo and terrible cell phone service.

Why didn't she tell us? Why didn't she wait?

Let's just say my visit was impulsive—an urge which I at first attributed to the suffocating deadness of an upstate New York winter, the hours holed up in my windowless studio, fully consumed by thesis work and attempting to teach undergraduates how to look at art. But I *know* it was something deeper—some sort of panic under the body current, a pull that was unmistakably biological, as if my DNA itself were communicating with me, drawing me westward, calling me back to her. I needed to fly home.

My visit would be a surprise—a quick trip of about four days. I'd see some friends in San Francisco, then hop on over to the East Bay to visit her. I thought it possible that an unplanned visit could excite her—force her from her comfort zones, her self-created limitations. The sight of my face would shock her into some accidental joy, even if just for a moment.

I still think my father must have, somehow, known.

A house is like a body. It has an interior, an exterior. A complex system of interworking parts. It stores things, holds things, deteriorates when deserted. It requires constant upkeep, becomes more and more familiar with time. A house is a massive living artifact, the most private of moments stored in the deep crevices of its creaking floorboards, in water stains and pencil marks, in tiny cracks in the ceiling, in chipped paint in the corners of rooms, in microscopic collections of dust and skin.

The Fifth Wall

Lathe, plaster, dropped ceilings, ductwork. Wiring and tendons, insulation and blood. You deconstruct a building in order to continue the lives of the materials, the purpose being to salvage the maximum amount of those materials for their highest and best re-use. It's all about the process. The collating and associating, the intention, the patterning.

The *and . . . action!*

Again, let's rewind.

It's the end of January, two days into my surprise trip. I borrow my friend Mallory's flashy ten-speed, which I carry onto BART to head over to my parents' house, only a short ride from the downtown station. It's an unseasonably warm day, thick with sunlight and a calm ocean breeze. I remember it so distinctly that it's almost like I'm back there on that day, entering the house with the bicycle over my shoulder. The bicycle is painted a neon pink and covered in glitter, with multicolored streamers dangling from the handlebars, and of course one of Mal's furry fabric trademarks sewn onto the frame. I turn the knob and the door's open, like it's always been on the weekends when my mother's home tending to the garden. I walk in sweating and panting from my recent lack of exercise; my thighs and calves are straining. I open the door and my mother's right there, poised in the foyer, facing a mirror, a gun in her mouth.

She's dressed normally, in jeans and a black crew-neck tee. Her hair is pulled up into a loose bun of faded gray-brown—I immediately notice that she stopped dyeing it blonde. I believe she is wearing canvas slippers.

I realize that I've never before seen an actual gun.

It happens in a second. I walk in and I see her, and for the life of me cannot remember and will never know, if she saw me or knew I was there, had heard me roll up on the stone pathway.

I open the door and the gun goes off and the bullet flies out the back of her and into the wall. Just like that. I hear the actual cracking of her skull. I watch both the gun and her body fall to the floor in a dead stillness. She pauses, drops, smacks on the floor. It sounds horrifically familiar, like a heavy schoolbag or a full laundry basket. Her body a heap of limbs reduced to weight. Dark blood pools around her, expands. It happens so fast that the moment is almost dissatisfying—like there should have been more build-up, more raw emotion, more immediate tension. Like the whole situation is somehow too real.

But the shock of the gun surprises me and causes me to jump back, which proves difficult because I'm still holding the bike, which I immediately drop, but because of its size and furriness and placement on my shoulder, it falls slanted, and the front wheel knocks me sideways. The whole bike crashes on top of me and twists my right knee to the point where I'm crying out more from the pain in my leg than from what I've just witnessed, which I still haven't fully processed yet, and which sends me into a whole new level of distress—guilt, untimeliness, self-hatred at my own clumsiness, unforgiveable, targeted self-pity. It turns the whole thing into an appallingly awkward moment. It confuses the subject of my reaction, prevents me from focusing.

I remember, while I lay on the floor, disheveled and sobbing from shock and embarrassment, smelling, suddenly, an over-whelming onslaught of her perfume. I remember thinking it doesn't make any sense that she is dead if I can smell something so distinctly familiar, so recognizable, so normal. It confused me because I couldn't recall smelling it before I fell down. I wanted to know how that could work scientifically—if when someone dies somehow their smell intensifies, rushes out of their pores or something. I needed it to make sense.

There was a fly buzzing in a corner of the foyer that would not for its life desist. I heard a TV on in the background, *the ideal consistency of cupcake icing.* The creaking hinges of the front door. Everything and nothing was keeping me from focusing.

The Fifth Wall

I wanted it to feel different. I wanted to feel more.

I remember lying there as the blood escaped and coagulated, formed a halo around her head—her face, at that point, still shielded from me, facing the wall, leaving my own body and seeing the scene from above, watching it and replaying it as if on a screen, judging myself and my actions, wishing to go back.

Perhaps I installed the camera because I know I'll want to recall the deconstruction later, as it actually happens, in real time. It's depressing how memory doesn't seem to be enough anymore. I need an image to verify what's happening outside of the screen.

"I thought your art was about *constructing* things," Mal says to me when I show her some of the footage. I'd dropped out of the program my last semester, subletted my apartment in Ithaca for a year, and moved in with Mallory in the Mission District.

Art, I shake my head at her. This is definitely not art. I ask how could it be? This is my real life that's happening. How can this possibly be art?

Just knowing that the house existed gave me terrible anxiety. I couldn't eat. I couldn't sleep. Masturbating was just out of the question. At work I almost spilled my coffee on a Takashi Murakami paper dress—I just walked right into the mannequin. I'd been picking up art preparator shifts at SFMoMA, where I worked all throughout undergrad. The principal exhibit tech— my boss, Robby, a longtime friend of my father—actually ordered me to take a nap in the conference room.

Something had to happen. Together, the house and I could not exist.

Now watch it come crashing down.

The house becomes a series of rooms, becomes compartmental units, becomes an arrangement of objects, becomes a composite

Rachel Nagelberg

of materials. It is a construction in reverse—you dismantle from the inside out.

It's like an autopsy.

I pick up the axe. Then everything disappears.

ACT ONE

The Real itself, in order to be sustained,
has to be perceived as a nightmarish unreal spectre.

SLAVOJ ZIZEK, Welcome to the Desert of the Real

some form of Alzheimer's, whom he didn't like to leave alone for more than a few hours, and the fresh air always calmed her. At some point he'd heard splashing and a high-pitched yelp, and he ran sprinting to the water to find old Maddie twenty feet deep into the river, unable to swim. He said his heart almost dropped out of his body. Without thinking twice, he rushed into the freezing cold after her, with clothes, boots, tools—everything—and reached her just as her legs gave out. Both of them panting, he pulled her towards the shore, threw her in the car, drove straight back to his house in the city and right into the hot shower—both of them shivering under the pressure and steam. He said nothing had ever terrified him more, nothing except for what had happened earlier that day, when I tore down the lawn towards my house, a giant axe raised in my palms like a crucifix.

I sensed less of a concern than a sparking interest. Jesse was gaping at me with an intensity I hadn't experienced before. Our playful flirting the past week had been merely a tease at most, nothing to this degree. He listened intently as I—still partially in shock—told him I still had no recollection of what happened before he tackled me to the ground. I recalled standing in front of the house in deep contemplation when all of a sudden a bizarre feeling came over me—all-consuming. It was like a severe case of déjà vu, where everything around me looked both familiar and foreign at the same time. Oddly depthless. As if the landscape was lacking something vital for me to process as "real." Jesse's weight had shifted closer to me, his concentration stark and aggressive. I quietly told him about the secret tumor, and then the gun. How I found my mother dead in the hallway. At least that's how I decided to tell it. I still haven't been able to admit the whole truth out loud. I must still have a lot of anger bottled up, I tried to joke, although it wasn't very funny. I'm always demeaning everything I feel strongly about. Is it out of some sort of embarrassment? Some flawed characteristic—a lack of conviction? It did concern me that that I had nearly killed myself with a very sharp, heavy object in some sort of unconscious state. I did distinctly remember waking up from it—seeing the actual fissures in the plaster in front of me, a heavy burning object in my hand, feeling a tight hold on my wrist. I remember that the heat was not from the axe but from my body's elevated temperature. I remember *rage* unlike anything I've ever experienced, a feeling so foreign to me, and yet shockingly exhilarating. I had felt dangerous, beautifully and horrifically alive. I wanted, consciously, to destroy, to completely obliterate. To kill. I knew I was being filmed.

I also knew, as I returned Jesse's gaze, that I was witnessing the innate attraction of this much older male to an acute madness inside me. It was a power I had felt only a handful of times. And I immediately loved it. Every second of it.

After one margarita I was smashed, but effectively hiding it, and we ordered two more and huddled closer together. Jesse, a young forty-seven, with a fit, trim body in his paint-splattered canvas Carhartt workpants and scuffed Timberlands—a dog lover with grit-encrusted nails, the energy of a stallion.

"Most people I work for want to build up," Jesse raised his muscular arms, "like the whole of civilization, always reaching for the stars. The nature of progress. But you—you called me and said *I want to unbuild, to alter the course of evolution.* I was like, who *is* this woman?"

I sipped my sour drink and smiled.

"You're lucky the house was beyond any sort of affordable repair. The termite damage was insurmountable. And the house was never fully secured onto its foundation in the first place—it would have been impossible to sell in its condition."

"Yes, we're doing everyone a favor," I said. "The materials that aren't damaged will become embedded into new projects in a continuous cycle of inevitable decay."

Jesse laughed. "Your morbidity is terribly sexy."

"The treacherous life cycle of a building—like a body with

thousands of organ transplants and plastic surgeries, being kept alive by machinery."

"I'm absolutely loving this."

"I'm glad somebody is."

"Most people take buildings for granted," he said. "They think of them as permanent fixtures—as if they weren't created by human hands."

"They create stability. They're always here, witnessing our lives."

"You wouldn't believe the panic attacks I've seen over trivial matters like a broken toilet, a hole in the roof, a basement leak... you'd think these people's lives were ending. And here you're literally taking it apart."

"Well, you're literally doing it. But yes, I'm extinguishing its power. Eradicating its history. There's a dangerous power to spaces. They hold certain energies, like bodies. They trigger memories. I mean—the idea of ghosts haunting houses has existed for thousands of years, in different cultures across the globe. I think there's something potent in this idea—in thinking about a house as a body-organism, a living structure designed to hold things, programmed for attachment."

"Okay, so I see you've thought through this all *theoretically*. But what does the rest of your family think about all this? Are they even in the picture?"

I told him about my parents' divorce when I was fifteen. How my dad, a tenured professor at Berkeley, lives now on a sailboat docked in Marin. For the past few years he's been making calculated steps to ultimately moving "off the grid"—what I see as just a glorified way of disappearing. He removed his name from the lease years ago—he and my mother having rarely spoken in the past decade. She lived in that house all alone. Then there's my brother, Caleb, who's been traveling in Peru for the past couple of years studying shamanic plant medicine with a tribe of indigenous Shipibos. We hear from him infrequently—usually in the form of heavy-handed emotional correspondence often emailed or texted directly after some drug-induced state. He flew home for the week of the funeral, and then hopped right back on a plane to Lima. And all my grandparents are dead, with some aunts and uncles scattered around the country living separate, private lives. I am pretty much a lone wolf.

"It's like you're living the movies," he snickered.

"Cinema does love the dysfunctional."

"Why'd your parents get divorced?"

"I think that when two emotionally unavailable people couple, it can either be oddly functional or disastrous."

Jesse moved in closer. "So what you're saying is that the sex was terrible."

"It always comes down to men and sex."

"What can I say? It's biological. We have absolutely no control."

This was a man who had six chickens, was known in his neighborhood for leaving fresh eggs on doorsteps in recycled cartons decorated by his four-year-old niece. He sat inches from me, his knee just barely grazing my shin. He radiated a vibrant youthfulness, smiling with his whole body, seeming to speak a special language embedded with playfulness, laughter. But his intensity was alarming. His deep interest felt genuine, but also as possibly that of a predator who preys on the weak—one who gets off on playing the role of the knight in shining armor. But he lifted a heaviness in me I realized right then I'd been carrying without feeling its full weight. It escaped from me like sand bursting from an hourglass, scattering around me with shards of broken glass. I felt light, buoyant, incredibly alive.

We both knew where the night was headed, but pretended to be blind. After another round and some horrible Ethiopian, I told him I wanted to meet his chickens, so we headed for his place—right around the corner, no doubt—with buzzing bodies exuding a sexual tension that was sure to be catastrophic.

From then on the images are blurry, violent, tequila-infused. It takes a few minutes to get the pee out from all the soreness. But there is relief in the pain, something dark, and joyous.

Back in my apartment, I pause the recorded footage. I take a deep breath, and then rewind about ten minutes. I press play.

There I am, standing motionless, with my back to the camera, the silhouette of my body outlined against the towering, faceless structure. I am a thin frame of near-translucent skin. Wind tousles my hair, whips through branches and grass. The elastic strap of the filter mask hugs the back of my hair; two plastic points of safety goggles stick out from behind my ears.

To see myself from a third eye point of view. This is the power of the camera.

Around me, the construction crew prepares for the removal of the house's non-load bearing walls. A few minutes pass where I do not move. There is something startling in seeing myself from this angle. Like witnessing something I'm not meant to see.

Oh, but here it begins—oh boy, is it coming. This scene is absolutely incredible. Academy Award-winning. Two thumbs up. It still gets me every time. All right, here we go. Watch it closely. At exactly TC 01:92:14:01 my right hand begins to stir. Do you see it? It's like watching Frankenstein's first awakening, or the hand of the wounded alien on the fanatical surgeon's table in *Independence Day*—when the camera shot zooms right in to the first sign of life, purposefully directs our focus to its movement. (A typical film strategy for creating tension—movement returns first to the extremities.)

Here, ladies and gentleman, is me, SHEILA. I point to the screen for an imaginary audience, and circle my body with a fluorescent yellow pen. And here, about two feet beside me, I tell them, is a stray PICKAXE, which I also circle, but in fluorescent blue.

My hand starts to shake, and soon my entire body. I look

like I'm convulsing. Perhaps it's the lack of transition between my near five-minute paralysis and the sudden awakening, or the sheer dissonance I feel with my image on the screen—but the shock of the moment is terrifying. I watch myself slowly bow my head down and spot the PICKAXE. There is a three-second pause. Suddenly I'm bent down and grasping it, lifting it over my shoulder and into the air—a crazed tyrant, a rabid executioner. I'm sprinting with this heavy object that I've never before used down a small grassy incline and across the front lawn past a bunch of busy workers who appear to be in the process of still figuring out that something is not quite right. Jesus Christ—I swing the PICKAXE into the first floor's outer wall. Look at how it breaks the skin and gets slightly caught, how I manage to pull it out, almost losing my balance, instead catching myself with a half-skip and wobble. It appears almost like a dance. Although I can't see my face, I am ninety-six percent sure that I'm displaying what is known notoriously as the *Sheila B. Ackerman Face*—the contorted, pained expression I can't help but make when I'm thinking hard, which happens often in class and also while creating art, and unfortunately, during sex, which often involves the guy asking if I'm all right, which can get fairly awkward at certain not-quite-the-right-moments. Watch me drive that fucker and hit the metal framing, which I can tell from afar because of the motion's hard, visible pause. From this distance—if you look really hard—you can also spot the cracking of the second story's SHEATHING, the slight shaking of the board above me, loosening with each blow. There is JESSE now, running towards me, waving his hands in the air and shouting, it looks like, although there is no sound.

I pause the video.

In the kitchen, Mal stands at the counter stirring a ceramic cup of Yerba Mate with her special metal straw. "Did you feel that five-point-seven this morning?" she asks, staring at her iPad.

"I woke up on a rocket ship," I say while typing *amnesia, paralysis, convulsions,* and *rage* into the WebMD symptom checker app on my iPhone. It's apparent she didn't hear me sneak in this morning.

"This article says we're in for a series of intense ones within the next couple of weeks."

"Is that right?" The website says *loading...*

"First the drought, and now this—the planet's obviously trying to tell us something."

Upon moving back to California, I'd been shocked at the desolation of the city—trees that normally brim with lush greens are now brown and sagging, lacking vibrancy, stunted in their natural bloom. A thin layer of dust shrouds all cars and buildings. The air feels drier, deader—a vast thirstiness you can feel deep inside your bones. San Francisco is turning into a desert.

"They expect the next one to be at *least* a five-point-nine." Mal covers her mouth.

"You better secure those jars."

Mal looks up and quietly contemplates the kitchen. "The *jars.*" Her eyes widen.

I pour some leftover hot water into a French press lined with local fair trade coffee we get discounted from Mal's barista friend, and watch the granules steep, while a screen the size of an index card loads all the possible medical threats to my living body. The kitchen looks like the combination between an apothecary and a meth lab. Alphabetically organized bottles of liquid herbal supplements line the counter along with stacked mason jars filled with soaking hemp seeds, raw nuts, lentils, and seaweed. There's a food processor, a dehydrating oven, two juicers, and a bullet blender. Atop the refrigerator a Saran-wrapped container of homegrown tofu sprouts next to a fermenting kombucha mother hovering in a massive glass bowl. Somewhere during the three years I'd been away Mal had met the Angel Granola and converted to an artistic practice of naturo-path*ology*. I open a non-GMO Snickers bar and pour my coffee.

Mal and I met in undergrad at Berkeley in a Foundations art class. This was during a third-wave-feminist phase of hers—years before Miley Cyrus' conversion—where she dressed in elastic onesies, platform shoes, and bleached her then long, wigishly thick hair as part of some grand, ironic public gesture of female assertion—a walking, talking caricature of herself. She worked in mediums of sculpture and performance, often creating works using solely untraditional materials, such as makeup, hair dye, and once even real menstrual blood in order to create what she called "authentic works of female desecration." I'll never forget modeling for her notorious Feminine Product Clothing line, my outfit composed of two hundred maxi-pads sewn together into a three-dimensional chastity belt, a push-up bra shaped with tampon applicators, and a set of diaphragm socks. I still sometimes use a photo from that show as my Facebook profile picture.

This past year has been a rough one for Mal as well. A gallery job she'd been working towards for quite sometime fell through, so she'd been forced to pick up more hours at an upscale pizza restaurant she'd been working at on and off since undergrad—a funny place to work for the now budding raw foodist. Then, with the rent doubling from the previous master tenant's surprise move-out, she'd had to quickly find a replacement who could afford the difference—a young but balding Delaware transplant named Dustin who programs some kind of drones for Google, wears baggy JNCO jeans, and drinks beet juice incessantly out of a plastic-lidded cup with a straw. In just a few years San Francisco has turned into a tech scene cesspool, where a studio price now starts at about $1600 per month, and most of our mutual artist friends have moved across the bay to Oakland—now also considered an "up and coming" area that's quickly becoming unaffordable. But Mal isn't ready to give up the vibrant, eclectic city life, nor the queer scene she's been involved with—formed an identity around—for years. Luckily I've moved back just in time to turn the awkward living situation into a threesome—we converted the old Victorian's dining room into a viable bedroom using two thick curtains and a few layered oriental rugs.

Mal met my mother a handful of times—had joined us once for a wine tasting weekend up north during one of my mother's unsuccessful attempts to have family time, a trip which proved to be a huge cover for my mother not knowing how to reveal to me that she had been asked to move to Paris by a former lover she'd recently reconnected with over the Internet (a "trained Ethnobotanist with a superior taste for French cuisine"), and that she was planning her move for that following spring. Of course that never actually happened, as the man turned out to be an ex-convict writing to her from a halfway house in Denver—which my mother luckily discovered before buying her ticket when mentioning his name to an old mutual friend—but a deep understanding had taken place there between Mallory and I, as she'd witnessed the extent of my mother's neurosis first hand. In other words, the deconstruction makes sense to her on some level—albeit she worries, I'm sure, that it's a lot more work—emotionally and physically—than it's worth. But Mal's not one to stop any project halfway; she's a proponent of taking anything to its end.

Peripheral neuropathy, transient ischemic attack (mini-stroke), hypoglycemia, intoxication, cocaine abuse—I scroll through the virtual hypochondria—*lead poisoning, epilepsy, premenstrual syndrome...*

Mal hops off the counter. Her short, matted bed-hair sticks up in outrageous places, though appears somehow purposeful, framing her face beautifully, perfectly effortless. Her bare, olive-toned arms and upper torso showcase many visible moles and warped stick-and-poke tattoos, faded and bleeding out from the years. "I'm planning on going up to another retreat at Harbin next weekend, so you'll have to keep an eye on these babies."

I stare at the jar-filled cardboard box groggily, caramel sticky in my teeth. "Since when did you become such a retreat junkie?"

"Since I met that woman 'Astral Sunflower' a few years ago and she opened my eyes to an invisible world of pure, potential happiness. And extremely hot women."

Multiple sclerosis, Lyme disease, weeverfish sting, cannibalism in Papua New Guinea. Weeverfish sting? Cannibalism in Papua New Guinea? I shut off my phone. "Isn't that the woman who gave you herpes?" I say.

She glares at me. "Sheila, everyone has herpes."

"I don't have herpes."

"You probably have herpes. They don't even test for it anymore."

"I sincerely doubt that, Mal."

"Look it up—," she reaches for my phone, "I'm telling you the truth, I swear!"

Dustin appears in the doorway wearing a Bluetooth headset, slurping a plastic cup caked with a day-old dried burgundy. I watch Mal slightly throw up in her mouth.

He grabs a half-eaten burrito from the refrigerator, speaking numbers quietly into the mic, and slithers back through the doorway.

"What do you even do at these retreats?" I sit at a counter stool and pour another coffee.

"Well, it depends on the retreat. This one's at a hot springs and is called *True Embodiment & the Realization of Self Truth.*"

"You know that title uses 'truth' twice."

Mal contemplates it for a second, and then shrugs.

"What does it even mean?" I ask.

"I mean, it's a bogus title, Sheils, but it's also pretty irrele-vant—it's like when a bad writer goes to see some really cool fucking art. If the art is legit, it transcends any wording catastrophes that try to box it in."

I sip my coffee and nod. An image of one Mal's first installations, *Gut Feelings*, comes to mind, where she arranged onto walls enclosed boxes of chicken livers and intestines tacked in various positions with hand-sized holes for daring audience members to stick gloved hands inside and feel around for the box's surprise.

I wonder what my organs would feel like if dissected and rearranged, mounted in dark space.

"Whatever you say," I shrug. "I know weird shit's bound to happen at gatherings like that."

"Weird shit happens all the time, everywhere, around the clock. Especially in this city. I mean, you're from Berkeley."

I give her *the look*.

"Okay, okay." She concedes, and sits down next to me. "There *was* this one retreat, a few years ago—it was only my second or third one. It was up at Mount Shasta and we were staying in our own separate yurts, men separated from women, of course. After a week, all of the women's yurts—mine included—started to *reek* of urine. We had absolutely no idea why this was happening—the outhouses were closer to the men's yurts, and we were using a ton of sawdust." She shakes her head. "Anyway, it turns out that one of the men was sneaking into all the women's yurts and leaving drinking glasses filled with his own urine underneath our beds—I'm guessing as some sort of fetishistic gesture of leaving his scent..."

"That's absolutely disgusting."

"I know."

"That's like, even weirder than anything I had possibly imagined you were going to say."

"Is it really?"

"Positively."

"Well, you know, I've learned to research a lot since then.

The Fifth Wall

It's like finding a gynecologist—you go to the one with the least amount of public lawsuits."

I lower my head in defeat.

"By and large, you are not one to judge, Sheila Bee." Mal wraps her arm around me, presses her warm cheek to my own, the sweet scents of peppermint and eucalyptus.

Her phone rings, the theme song to *Strangers with Candy*. Her aggression is quick and piercing on the phone, as if continuing a heated conversation put on hold. A wild persona reserved for specific people, times, places. "All I'm saying is I got a weird feeling, lady. Plus he doesn't want to have sex with you, which is *hot*." She motions for the doorway. "And your vagina is like Neverland—she loves the lost boys."

Outside, the wind from the bay rips across telephone poles, knocks over garbage bins, thrusts between buildings in high-pitched resonances. The homeless poke through clinking glass bottles to sell back to the closest Safeway. A muscular woman leads a group of five children down the sidewalk all wearing dark sunglasses. A man walking by shouts HOW ARE MOMMY'S TEETH? into a Bluetooth. Beneath California, the Earth's crust is preparing to release energy into shattering, seismic waves. The soil is preparing for its transition into sand. The Earth speaks, the city shudders. The smell of Southern Indian leaks through the vents.

An unsettling feeling fills my stomach. That feeling I felt yesterday in front of the house—that depthlessness that came over me, that extraordinary sense, that *lack*—like a swallowing. Nothing that I can categorize into a WebMD symptom app. The house, pulling me inside its time warp of trauma. *It's not enough to die. You still have to disappear.* I read somewhere that in some surviving ancient Mayan cultures, the body of the deceased is sat upright in the shared main space of the family's household for days, weeks, and sometimes months, so that they can witness the process of decay—the skin, sinew, and muscle

Rachel Nagelberg

sliding from bones, the process of decomposition a communal spectacle, a collective visual mourning—the townspeople often speeding up the process by eating its flesh and meat. These practices are seen as the first burials, the liminal states between life and death. After the body decays, the second burial takes place, where the bones are then buried in the ground, often underneath the floor of the immediate household, becoming literally embedded into its history.

The archaeologist who wrote the article visited this particular culture to observe this extraordinary death ritual. There, a townsperson asked him to account for burials in America, to explain the process of our transition from death to the next world. The archaeologist tried to explain embalming, but before he could even finish, the Mayan turned to the side and vomited, refusing afterwards to talk any more with any members of the team. The archaeologist supposed that the man was so offended by American practices, that he couldn't even bear to accept their weight. The American Dream: to make the living dead look alive.

But to watch a loved one's body decompose—at first it seems more honest. To really know and witness death as a part of life. It only seems natural. But where is the ritual when a dense black ball of matter spreads its icy fingers into one's brain cavities without warning? Where is the ritual in suicide?

We had my mother cremated. Right after the small funeral, per her instructions (in a will she'd written and notarized a few weeks prior to her death), Caleb, my father, and I flew with her contents to an old horse farm in Ottsville, Pennsylvania, where her parents used to send her to camp in the summers. Apparently that was her favorite place in the world. None of us ever knew.

A German artist, Gregor Schneider, recently released an ad for a volunteer to spend his or her last living days in a museum space. He wants to sequester a dying individual in the confines of four white public walls and display his or her last moments to all. In an interview he said that he wanted to display a person dying naturally, in peace. That he didn't understand why death couldn't be a positive experience, why it's such a complication to portray the beauty of death, to create human places for the dying and dead. People send him death threats.

There's a three-second segment in a home video I salvaged in which my mother says something to the camera that I can't quite make out. I've replayed it a countless number of times, to the point of an obsession I'm not quite yet readily able to admit. The film furrows and chafes; black and white lines zigzag along the cascading color image, light and dark grays forming up and down its quivering surface. From behind the camera, my dad asks her a question. He zooms in until her face fills the screen. My mother has one of those kinds of mouths that curl up to the side when she talks. She smiles and tilts her head a degree or two and says something to the camera and blinks. But her voice drowns out from the static on the tape.

It is a machine that walks, runs, climbs, and carries—a sleek, four-legged assemblage of algorithmic, interlocking parts. Headless and faceless, but with a computer as its brain. An engine as its spirit. Named the "Drog" by its creator in reference to its dog-like proportions and its drone-robotic technology, the machine is considered "intelligent," can navigate a wide variety of terrains. There are sensors for locomotion, joint position, joint force. Planning, actuation, pose estimation, control. It has a GPS, stereo vision system, lidar, and gyrosope. Proprioception, exteroception, homeostasis. This is a machine that can see on its own.

"Four feet long, three feet high. This girl's about the size of a Rottweiler." The artist chats while an AV tech tries to get a sense of the Drog's electronics to sync with the other pieces in SFMoMA's new upcoming show, *The Last Art*. I stare at the artist while taking measurements for a custom barricade around the scary-looking thing for protection—whether for the Drog or for the public, I'm not exactly sure.

Behind the scenes, the museum is bustling with at least three times as many bodies due to the complex technological nature of the show. They brought their own exhibition and AV techs, plus thirteen different curators to work in tandem with our own curators, preparators, and electricians. We've begun to start referring to this setup as "the war room."

"Its custom GPS allows for 'human following'—you know, device drivers, data logging, visual odometry. We have sensors focusing directly on its internal state, monitoring the hydraulics, oil temp, battery charge, etcetera." The artist is tall and lanky with dark inset eyes and pale, freckled skin. His nametag says Michael Landy. I can't stop staring at his face. There's something about him that looks just like Adam Black.

Michael Landy looks toward me, and I immediately resume focusing on my menial task at hand. Out of the corner of my eye, I glimpse the Drog in an uncanny seated position against the far wall, not yet activated. I feel the artist's shadow approach me.

"Nice gloves," he says, eyeing me.

I immediately look around me, my favorite gesture of pretending to be blind. "Who, me?"

He laughs. White gloves are mandatory for everyone in this room. He stands over me, silently.

"What's . . . up?" I ask awkwardly. The AV tech rolls his eyes.

Michael Landy observes the chalked line I've been making around the Drog's allotted roaming space. "You know in the labs we just let this baby run free."

"Is that right?" I pretend to be busier than I am, studying the tape measure intensively and double-marking off lines. The resemblance to Adam is less in his face than his overall bone structure, his authoritative stance. The unadulterated, academic sureness.

"Yeah we have this little compound in L.A. We're working on a whole Noah's ark of machines that use drone technology to see, hear, and feel."

"Will they all be headless?" I ask.

He laughs. "No, definitely not. This model is based on a military funded prototype invented a few years ago at MIT to take the place of humans in hazardous environments. But here we've stripped away the military context and are presenting the first introduction of this kind of automata into a gallery space. How do we look at this kind of technology as art? is the kind of question we're after."

"What does it mean to see without eyes?"

The Fifth Wall

"Precisely," he says, moving closer. A smirk forms on his lips. "Or—rather—what is a *visionless* gaze?"

The Last Art—a machine that sees for itself. What else could be left—a machine that dreams?

Michael Landy continues to observe me with a new interest I immediately recognize. My body starts to grow excited. I realize that right here, in this room, I'm holding all the power. The artists aren't even allowed to touch their own work.

A timer goes off on my phone. In ten minutes there's a mandatory team meeting about the museum's acquisition of a multimillion-dollar Richard Serra sculpture—one of his infamous "torqued ellipses" entitled *Band*. It's scheduled to open with *The Last Art* in three weeks. I begin to pack up my tools.

"I expect I'll be running into you in the near future," says Michael Landy, grinning, and walks back over to the AV tech handling his Drog.

I feel a slight shift of energy in the room, as if the world around me is rearranging. A hollowness forms inside of my body, but also a heightened sensation, a buzzing of attraction from the interest of this strange, yet uncannily familiar man.

I hadn't seen Adam Black in over four years—and he was hardly on any social media. We met in my Introductory Film class freshman year, which he'd taught—a young PhD candidate in film studies, from whom I suffered years of romantic obsession after a drunken encounter at a party. I'd sent him a long, esoteric email during my first semester of grad school, which he never responded to. Our whole nonexistent relationship had from the beginning suffered from multiple bouts of intellectual intensity patterned with long absences of nothing—no communication—at all.

I've found that when you build up a fantasy, it tends to become stronger than the memory, strangling it to asphyxiation; it takes over the past. Adam Black: a figure ever since fixed indefinitely as the image of my absent lover.

On my way to the conference room, I stop to read a blurb about *The Last Art* tacked to a makeshift wall in the gallery:

THE LAST ART PRESENTS AN INTERACTIVE VENUE TO EXPERIENCE INNOVATIVE TECHNOLOGY AS WORKS OF CONTEMPORARY ART. WHAT IS THE DIRECTION THAT ART IS MOVING IN? WHAT KIND OF HISTORICAL PERIOD DO WE FIND OURSELVES IN, NOW THAT WE'VE HISTORI- CIZED EVERYTHING UP TO THE PRESENT MOMENT? WITH THE FLOODING ADVENT OF NEW TECHNOLO- GIES THAT ALLOW USERS TO ARCHIVE LIFE AS IT'S HAPPENING, WE FIND THAT CONTEMPORARY ART IS BECOMING A WAY OF ARCHIVING THE PRESENT—THE IDEA THAT NOT ONLY CONTEMPORARY ARTISTS ARE ARCHIVISTS, BUT ALL WHO USE TECHNOLOGY, FOR WE ARE CONSTANTLY RECORDING LIFE AS IT IS HAPPENING. EVERYTHING IS HAPPENING *LIVE*. FROM HANDHELD RECORDING DEVICES AND GPS SYSTEMS TO VIRTUAL REALITY INTERFACES, SELF-DRIVING CARS, BIOTECH- NOLOGICAL ANIMAL PROTEIN GROWTH, AND MECH- ANIZED ORGANS, WE HAVE ENTERED INTO A PERIOD WHERE WE NO LONGER NEED BODIES TO MOVE, OR EYES TO SEE. NOW THAT THE BOUNDARIES BETWEEN ART, SCIENCE, AND TECHNOLOGY ARE BECOMING EVER- BLURRED IN THEIR ATTEMPTS TO IMAGINE NEW POS- SIBILITIES FOR THE FUTURE, WHAT WILL THE ERA OF THE POSTHUMAN HAVE IN STORE FOR US, AND FOR ART? WHAT WILL THE ROLE OF ART TAKE ON?

Printed below is an image of a sheep as the show's advertised icon. It refers to the sculpture *Dolly*, a life-size replica of the infamous first living clone, Dolly the Sheep. It's by the same artist famous for crystallizing an inoperative missile from the Iraq War.

The Fifth Wall

Several minutes are all that remain of man. The line comes back to me from a podcast I listened to on the bus over here—a former designer of nuclear weapons on NPR. *It's no longer in our hands.*

How could it be—in our society, where we go to the movies to view its own destruction as an aesthetic experience—that we're still blind to the real life possibility of our own instantaneous deaths?

I think of the camera I've mounted in front of the deconstruction, surveilling 24/7 the dismantling of my childhood home—this window I've opened onto this dreadful process.

Perhaps it's not that we romanticize our own destruction, but that we *have* to fantasize about it in order to understand it. That in this world now dominated by screens and images, we must stage massive fictions in order to live.

Light pours into the conference room from four floor-to-ceiling length windows, spreads a sheerness over a central oblong granite table, leather executive axis chairs. Seven of us fill the seats with an unfocused mid-afternoon Monday energy, slumped and yawning in front of to-go paper coffee cups amidst a scattered arrangement of recyclable cardboard sleeves. A handful of others line the walls behind us, a slight murmur filling the room.

On the far wall, Robby projects a video of Richard Serra's *Band* in its initial exhibit at the New York MoMA in 2006. The sculpture looms before us, a gigantic and endless plane of movement, its form a twisted anatomy of a chocolatey-casted, weatherproof steel. Rising about twelve-and-a-half feet high and almost seventy-two feet in diameter, the surrealistic, slithering ribbon is a contorted rectangular strip on its side, an undulating band of one curvaceous body. From below, the camera focuses on *Band*'s concave façade, which appears windswept; it gives the illusion of an unfixed medium, like cotton, canvas, or felt. It defies any natural or architectural shape.

Robby has one of those soft, malleable faces where the skin around the edges hangs loosely from bone. He has a relatively thin frame—small arms and legs, though a bit of a protruding stomach. He carries himself with a sophisticated clarity, has what I've come to associate as a strictly European-American trait: the ability to transform physical imperfections into attractive characteristics—knobby elbows, elongated torso, crooked teeth—though he dresses in faded cotton tees and loose, ripped jeans. Style versus comfort: an artist-technician conundrum. I've known Robby since my birth, he and my father having attended Stanford together, and both part of some elite intellectual boys club that met once a month over drinks and cigars to discuss critical theory and the state of postmodernism. My father, a budding dramatist, and Robby, then, a painter, both now living out the aftermaths of academic idealism with working class jobs and cirrhotic livers.

"As you can probably tell, there is no way in *fuck* that thing's coming in here in one piece. There will be a series of loading trucks carrying sections we'll unload into the lower atrium through the two forty-foot garage doors, each piece weighing about twenty tons total." Robby pauses the video and points to a loose map of the building drawn onto a dry-erase board, his beady blue eyes lit and bulging from some portion of his daily ten cups of gunpowder green tea. He traces the path of assembly with his finger.

"There is, unfortunately, always an issue setting up Serra's sculptures." Robby crosses his arms. "One that I wanted to discuss in the sculptural curator's presence, but considering she's running a little late," he studies his watch again for obvious effect, "I might as well go ahead and start."

Legs shake. Fingers tap. Somebody sneezes.

"Richard Serra," Robby says, slowly weaving his fingers together, "is a dick."

A tired communal chuckle erupts from the half of us who

know this spiel already—one of Robby's infamous "insert notorious artist" cautionary tales.

"And I'll tell you why," Robby says, sitting down and crossing his legs. "A few years back at the Legion of Honor, my close buddy Phil, one of the ranking techs at Atthowe Fine Art Services, was hired to rig and install Serra's *House of Cards*, which if you don't know already, but should, is a balancing box-structure of four very heavy, lead antimony plates." He crosses his legs and leans back, places his hands atop his belly. The chair croons. "Now, after analyzing the situation, Phil decided that for safety reasons, the piece needed invisible spot welds tacked in the upper corners of the plates. However, this apparently incensed the collector, who demanded that Phil remove them immediately. And Phil, being a hard-working and highly intelligent technician told the fucker *absolutely not*, and excused himself from the project. The deputy director then ordered a bunch of interns to remove the bracing, and can you guess what happened?"

"Human sandwich," I say.

"Try human vegetable," says Robby, and my chest tightens. "Of course, one of the plates isn't balanced correctly and falls on the poor kid, who hits his head on the floor and is in a coma for three months before the parents pull the fucking plug."

"Spoken quite candidly," a woman scoffs behind me.

Robby holds out his hands, shrugs comically. "The man is a psychopath. But *fuck*, is his art brilliant." He then passes out contracts that depict an agreement between us and the collector that we can abide by all the safety procedures that Robby and Derek, the head tech for Atthowe they're bringing in to help set up, tell us to perform. We all sign amidst buzzing, restless bodies preparing to disperse.

After the meeting, Robby and I walk to the break room in search of free pastries he'd heard rumored earlier that day. He asks how I'm doing. He attended the funeral, which is where

I'd asked him with sudden desperation about a job. He'd talked HR into letting me return as a preparator, but with some extra roles only if I want them—some kind of optional managerial status. Job descriptions in the art world are always sort of vague. He'd kept in touch with my mother even after the divorce. I tell him that I'm fine, considering that he knows nothing about the house, and I want it to stay that way.

"I talked to your father over the weekend—he asked after you. I told him you were my right-hand lady. How good it is to have you back." He pats me lightly on the shoulder. We stand in the sunlight holding paper plates piled with pastry remnants.

I nod. I tell him I haven't even seen my dad since the funeral. And he's never been much of a phone talker. He did send me a used copy of Nietzsche's *The Birth of Tragedy* in the mail—what I took as a thoughtful gesture, but of course wholly missing the point. Living on that sailboat has brought his isolation to a new level.

Robby sighs. He isn't naive about my dad's reclusive tendencies. "You know I'm here if you ever need anyone to talk to." I smile and nod. We munch the overly sweetened bread in silence.

hits, abruptly like a kind of violence. Though I've never quite figured out how to navigate it. I always went home after school to unwind; having time and space to myself was essential, a block in the day for my body to process. And I was a very emotional child—always reacting with high ups and downs. Rarely did I ever feel peaceful—always heightened with a forceful, manic energy, or deeply filled with doubt and unrest, lost in massive questions about life's meaning, feeling alien and isolated from others in my vast inability to be *in* life. Perhaps this is why I still cling to the camera; I've always been watching myself from afar.

Emotions from others would just bleed into me; especially my mother's—when she was upset, I'd *feel* it. And she was often upset. The most trivial disturbances in life horrified her to points of near madness. My father called it "Deirdre Syndrome"—this emotional upheaval, her apparent biological state of becoming lost in seconds. Her instantaneous reaction to the realization that she, ultimately, in the grand scheme of things, had no control. It's like she always felt crowded. She constantly needed space and yet, in that space she'd distract herself with technology. Soap operas and sitcoms and detective shows, computer Scrabble, Minesweeper, and other thought-numbing games. Her modes of distraction advanced when my father left, and reached a whole new level once Caleb and I left home. The whole house became appalling. Its necessary upkeep dwindled; various rooms were consistently in the midst of construction, picked up and dropped by either her or various Internet boyfriends; you felt like you were walking into a ruin. Wallpaper that had begun tearing fifteen years ago ripped off into strips and peeled from the walls like hanging flaps of colored skin. Throughout the years she'd acquired cats she rescued from the local shelter (upon cleaning out the house I'd discovered five, and quickly gave them away to neighbors), which clawed up the backs of chairs and furniture to frayed messes. A layer of cat hair coated all objects. Cat beds, cat toys, cat scratchers, empty

The Fifth Wall

cardboard boxes and bags for the cats to play in. A stranger upon walking inside might think it was a house for cats, with a person inside of it walking from screen to screen. The television and computer screens got bigger and bigger, and each visit it seemed like she sat closer and closer. By the end they were colossal. Tabletops stacked high with murder mystery and romance novels, local newspapers, popular women's magazines. It's as if the material world became secondary to the methods of distraction. The inhabitant moved from one station to the next. The in-between time proved a highly uncomfortable period, bearable only with prescribed marijuana and sparkling white wine on ice. All the furniture was pushed out from the wall in order to not touch the cords that ran behind it—trained by the hypochondriac of the family, my father, who would spend hours checking the house for possible fire hazards before we left for vacation, who once turned us around and backtracked two hours because he thought he left the toaster oven plugged in. The house, for him, seemed more like a responsibility than a refuge. The chaos of possible problems that existed outside of his study, where he'd spend hours reading Aristotle and Bataille into late hours of the night, lost in his own critique, the ice chinking in his tumbler that I heard from my bedroom while trying to fall asleep. The white noise from the television. My father would unwind from a semester by taking a few days to himself, in which he'd unplug and drive up the Northern coast with nothing but a pocketknife and a few other bare essentials, disappearing into the wilderness. This kind of "losing" of one's self terrified my mother; in the beginning I think she found his sovereignty attractive—probably kept him close to have that kind of power near—but in the end, couldn't break her fear of living, raised herself by working class parents in New York who lived through the Great Depression—I have early memories of my grandmother at restaurants shoving empty water glasses and ketchup packets into her purse—my mother never

47

At home, I check the live deconstruction cam and watch Jesse pulling drywall with two shirtless, perspiring Mexican men. We've planned another rendezvous for later this evening—I'll bring over a fancy pizza from Mal's restaurant, and he'll supply the beer.

With a couple hours of daylight left, I decide to take a short walk to the bustling part of the Mission to the restaurant, to have an early drink at the bar. The air outside is cool and brisk, but tolerable without a jacket. Clouds move swiftly above buildings, the sun appearing and disappearing like lightening, a false threat of rain. I arrive around five, just as they're opening up. Inside, Mal's behind the counter pressing her uterus against the pizza warmer. She spots me out of the corner of her eye.

"Industrial heating pad," she smirks.

I sit down and she pours me an oversized glass of Barbera. The wine tastes thick, fruity, and delicious. She sucks on an olive, looking bored. I tell her about the Drog and *The Last Art* exhibit. How everyone's talking about it being the most controversial show the museum's ever hosted. Mal says she'd seen an article for it in the Chronicle just last week. She'd had a nightmare that evening about Dolly the Sheep. Dolly hadn't been a sheep at all, but a costume that her aunt pulled off during a dinner party. The dinner had then gone on as usual dinners go. She had no idea what it meant.

I hadn't been remembering my dreams for years. But they started returning right after the suicide. They began as flashbacks of the shocking moment when I opened the door—the gun would go off, she'd fall to the floor, and then the bike would

49

fall on top of me and I'd wake up. But recently they've begun to shift. Each time the scenario twists, time shifts, and my past memories seem to mingle with the event to create a whole new scene altogether.

As the wine begins to set in, I feel my body altering to a space of slightly more detachment. I smile, feeling hot blood flowing through my veins.

Mal rushes from the kitchen and serves a large steaming pizza to a table of two. She walks back over to the bar.

"Check this out." She thrusts her iPhone in my face, and I examine the brightly lit screen.

"*The becoming of human,*" I read aloud, "—*unlike all other images or fakes, runs via a culture of total control. This strange desire, marooned in the abysmal darkness of this city—I am nothing, you are nothing. This is something we understand. This is our only armor.*" I look up from the screen. "The Oracle's having a good day."

Mal shrugs and quickly slips the phone back into her pocket. For the past five or six months, Mal's been receiving unsourced text messages from the same phone number, which we've named "the Oracle." They arrive erratically, often skipping days or weeks, in paragraph-long stanzas brimming with ontological desperation, never demanding a response, as if calling out from a void of electric currents, of sonic depths. They seem to at once predict the future, indicate the present, and symbolize the past. She's begun to trust in them—messages that seem to come from no one and are written to no one, but are—despite intention—*for her*. I'd Googled the number—a Manhattan area code. She once tried to call it but it just rang and rang.

She pours me a second glass of wine, this time a Chianti. "It's like I can't remember my life before the Oracle."

"You can't imagine living without him," I say.

"Or her," she says.

"Or her," I repeat. "Or it. Who says it has to be human?"

The Fifth Wall

A man walks into the restaurant and takes a seat at the bar beside me. Mal smiles and hands him a menu. She pours ice water into his glass, and then curses under her breath—she keeps forgetting she's not supposed to serve water anymore unless the customer asks, and plus she's already on thin ice, due to the other week when she got written up for ranting to a customer about the degenerative qualities of consuming gluten—obviously not the best selling point in a restaurant that makes all its dough off of *dough*. The man sitting next to me turns to me and smiles. Mal runs to check on a table aggressively waving their hands.

"Robert," the man announces, holding out his hand. I shake it, frowning.

"You look even more stunning in person," he says.

I stare at him with great confusion. I have no idea who this man is. I look around for Mal, but she's cleaning up a spill at a table.

"What a trip, getting here." He thumbs the laminated menu in a clockwise motion. Wire glasses frame his long, thin face. His short, dry hair a dark brown specked with gray. His other features are indistinguishable. "I'm so glad I made it on time. On the way driving over, I almost ran into a deer! A *deer*—I'm telling you, but it was already dead. It was in a heap in the middle of the street. I was coming from a job down in the Peninsula—it was right near the turn-off on 280. Just a big, old heap. And it was pretty fresh—not too much blood or anything. And it was weird—nobody else was around, no people walking, no cars. It's pretty rare—a deer in the city. I hadn't seen a deer in a long time. You know, I used to do a bit of taxidermy with my pops growing up. So I just decided, you know, why not just take it? Why don't I just hoist this baby into my trunk and put it in the walk-in cooler at work tomorrow morning?" The man looks at me and grins.

I stare at him. "There's a dead deer in your car."

Rachel Nagelberg

"I know, how funny is that!" He laughs and looks down at his menu.

Mal hurries to the bar looking exhausted. "Fucking Alexa just called in sick. I'm so tired of this bullshit." I drain the last of my wine and slam the empty glass down in front of her.

She glares at me. The dead deer man says he'll have what I'm having. She studies him, then looks at me. I give her *the look*.

She pours us both a glass of Chianti and leaves the open bottle on the counter, rushing back towards a dinging bell from the kitchen.

"You know taxidermy's a dying art form. You got these new age people all obsessed about the implications of hunting— I mean, don't get me wrong—these days I think ideally you should either hunt to eat the meat or find the exotic creature dead—but there's little respect for the art of preservation that goes into really high-quality taxidermy. There's something about experiencing the girth of an animal in its real flesh. You can *feel* its power. Sure, we have those nature planet shows—the places those cameras go! Amazing stuff." The man laughs. "But you can't feel a real presence from a TV show, you know? So what looks good on this menu, anyhow?"

My head feels dizzy. A throbbing develops in my temples. A woman approaches the bar wearing a long wool coat and dark, red lipstick. She looks around aimlessly, then spots the man beside me.

"I'm so sorry I'm late!" she says.

"Excuse me?" The man looks perplexed. He looks at me, and then back at her. His eyes widen.

"Rebecca?" he asks.

The woman extends her hand.

I drain the wine and leave immediately. The cold bay air stings my face and neck.

Pizza malfunction, I text Jesse on the curb. *Need assistance.* HELP!

The Fifth Wall

Meet at my place, he writes back. *Running late. Door should be open.*

I hop on the 19 Muni toward Potrero, a living, breathing mass. We climb on and we climb off, the bus stops and releases, consumes, moves forward, stops and releases, consumes us. The sounds of creaking plastic seats, rubbing nylon material, shuffling footsteps. A woman sitting behind me depicts a violent rape scenario in a conversation with herself. A plastic bottle rolls up and down the aisles. A young man coughs brutally into his sleeve.

Fucking dead deer in trunks. The wine surges through my bloodstream.

Jesse's sweet old dog, Maddie, greets me at the door with an awkward wobble. Then she bangs her head against the wall. I feel like crying.

Jesse's house is large and drafty, filled with mismatched furniture, tools, and dog hair. I run my fingers along the smooth granite kitchen counter lined with a gorgeous repurposed wooden trim.

I pull out a Pacifico from his fridge and sit on the sofa. I take off my shoes. I lay out on the sofa. I prop myself up with my elbow in a more attractive position. I wait. What kind of person leaves their door unlocked in this city? Especially with this senior citizen. I gape at Maddie, who sniffs my foot repeatedly. Then she hobbles over to a floor cushion and smacks her body to the ground. Sounds emanate from the door. I stand up.

Jesse walks in with a great energy. His grin exceeds the walls of the room. I fling myself at him.

He boils pasta and cooks a homemade mushroom sauce that smells heavenly as I pace around him telling him about my day—the Drog, the dead deer man, the crazy people on the bus. It's been just over twenty-four hours since the incident with the pickaxe and already the whole world feels like it's shifted to

Rachel Nagelberg

some disproportionate degree, and I am somehow in the center, spiraling, attracting destructive forces and energies orbiting around me like planets.

He had an interesting experience today, too, he says. The reason he was late is because he stopped by IKEA on the way home to pick up some cheap bathroom mats for his sister. He was rushing through the store—it was about to close—when he came upon a pregnant woman having a panic attack in a corner of the bathroom section. Apparently she'd been trying to find the exit for hours, but the store kept leading her to different rooms—the poor woman couldn't escape! He left the mats and helped lead the shaking woman out of the store to her car, where he sat with her for a few minutes making sure she was okay. She'd left her cell phone in the car, along with her emergency granola bar, which she inhaled while Jesse patted her back until she was ready to drive home.

I tell him how IKEA uses a specific type of coercive architecture designed to force you through the entire building before you can exit. That there are a bunch of interesting essays written about it on JSTOR. He says it sounds like it's right up my alley.

Later, after we fuck on the bench to the kitchen table, I lay awake buzzing in the arms of Jesse, while he snores with the mysterious sounds of an old man. A calm, collectedness washes over me, a sense of security. Asleep, Jesse is just a breathing body. All of his energy is contained in this one action—the pure, peaceful gesture of breath. His shin rests against my calf; my face nestles against his clavicle—time slows down to merely the placement of bodies. Nothing else exists but the two of us.

In my dream, I walk into a house that's not my mother's real house, but it's familiar and I recognize it as my own. It's dark outside and there are lights on in the house but not overhead lights—more like candles or low-wattage lamps—because the house is very dim-lit with shadows protruding out from all corners of the rooms. There's something eerie and absent about the house, something *cold*, though I don't recall feeling any sort of temperature or even what I am wearing or not wearing, and now that I think about it, one of the most startling details is the lack of definition between the outside and the inside of the house, like the only differentiation between the two is my recognition of the house's basic structure, because I walk in and the only real details I distinctly recall noticing are the wooden floorboards that cover the entire vicinity. So I'm walking through the rooms and am overcome with a sense of terror, as if suddenly my body knows where I'm going and why I'm going there but it's for some reason forgotten to tell my mind, so I'm picking up my pace now, and almost jogging through incalculable space until I get to what I recognize as the family living room. I drop to the floor and start prying open the floorboards with my hands. I am frantic and unstoppable, I am heaving with each breath. The floorboards tear away easily as if they know of my intentions and approve of them, and I realize that I've been screaming something since I entered the house, but I can't make out the actual words, only the shrieking, and finally a handful of floorboards are piled beside me as I gape down into the hole at my mother's naked body splayed out in front of me seeming as heavy as a large block of marble. I make out my screams now

Rachel Nagelberg

as, "Jesse! Jesse! Jesse!" because he's running in now to find out what's the matter, but he stops before he gets to me and gives me this look like *Sheila, what are you doing? What have you done?* and my eyes must be fucking swollen because I can hardly see through all of the liquid and I just don't understand, and I feel some sort of movement beneath me so I look down and my mom's head has started to move. Her head reanimates, but the rest of her body lies still. I can't remember actually seeing or recognizing her face, but just somehow knowing that it was her, and I'm not even exactly sure what she told me, but I remember it being something like assuring me that it was okay and to please just let her die, and my body just can't take it anymore—I'm shifting my neck back and forth from Jesse to my mom from Jesse to my mom and I think I'm screeching at Jesse why's he just standing in the corner, how he can possibly just let this happen—and then what happens last is why I no longer trust my own mind—I gasp because my mother's limp and exposed body is splitting like cells into two identical entities and one is rising above the original like some sort of spirit, and the head on the first one is still twitching autonomously while the second body, also naked and not dead, but not alive either because both bodies seemed somehow warm, lingers above, and before I know it Jesse has pushed me aside and is reaffixing the floorboards as I'm staring in horror at him and his motions and at the situation in general and wondering where my dad and brother could possibly be with all of this going on and if I'll ever stop shaking.

In the five or so minutes in the recorded footage where I appear to be paralyzed in front of my mother's house, there are two frames towards the middle of that time period that, when slowed down and examined closely, indicate a visible shift of some sort. Even from behind, my body, from the first frame to the second frame, appears wholly different—alert and clenched in a foreign way, charged differently, even from the screen.

It's like I turn into someone else.

Four days later, on Friday at 9 A.M., the Drog is reported missing; we all receive a massive text from Robby asking to report
any sightings immediately, and that we should continue our
work day as usual. At 10 A.M. one of the curators reports seeing
it bolt out of the Fisher Room and run down the hall towards
the central atrium. Following is a text from Robby confirming
that the machine is apparently turned *on*, but that it's nothing to freak out about—that it's just having some sort of minor
malfunction where it isn't responding to commands. So much
for that barricade.

This morning I've been busy hunting down a seagull that
accidentally flew into the main atrium. After hours of searching, a coworker and I found it nested in an installation by Shea
Hembrey called *Whirl*, a makeshift black hole of straw swirling
into the depths of the museum floor. We had to quickly get a
hold of *Whirl*'s collector, who happened to be vacationing in a
remote sector of Cuba, in order to get permission to step onto
the intricately placed stacks. It was all a huge mess of ridiculous formalities. An elderly gentleman watched the whole
rescue mission from the sidelines, laughing hysterically while
repeatedly slapping his knee.

Today is also the ninth day of the deconstruction, the day of
cutting roof trusses and disassembly. Since the situation with
the pickaxe—or *the Lack*, as I've been referring to it—I've begun
to assign myself to the position of viewer, utilizing the camera

as my only eyes. There is a power in the immediacy of access. The ability to see without being seen. Like looking into a crystal ball and seeing into the future.

And I have to admit—I find it fascinating to watch myself lose control—when I bolt down the front lawn. The sharp, gleaming metal.

It's not an uncommon fixation these days. I read that, when American soldiers found bin Laden, he was watching himself on television. I also read that, just recently, in Spain, a government protest was held using holograms of the protesters.

The real power exists in the images we create of ourselves.

Though yesterday I still went to the site with Jesse, promising not to pick up any tools. I examined the rotting wooden tie beams and rafters, the smell of mildew and earth and dust. The deconstruction's reached a level where all familiarity has left the building, reduced to a combination of woods and metals, a skeleton of materials.

After only a few months back in the Bay, I now feel completely wrapped up in its cosmic forces—the reality of my life in Ithaca already faded into the distance, as if a whole other world, invisible, but continuous, existing simultaneously alongside of this one.

Who *am* I now, in this city, without the stonewall structure of an east coast Ivy League campus, the status of *Classroom Instructor*, of *MFA Candidate*? I haven't been making real art in months, and it's becoming difficult to envision myself in this new role. Not that I was making a ton of installations over there. I've never subscribed to the idea that an artist needs to constantly produce—art is a state of mind, not a series of products.

How quickly the world around us rearranges.

In less than a week, Jesse and I've already formed a dynamic that's become repetitive. A non-discussed etiquette of dinner involving at least two drinks, for which he always pays, before the inevitable rabbit-fucking, followed by his almost immediate

Rachel Nagelberg

passing out—the hours I then lay awake already losing their potency, their power. The lack of infatuation, of romance—what before felt like desire, but now just an innocent, routine, before-bedtime affair.

The truth is I'm becoming bored.

Thomas Francis Scott (b. 1979)
The Future is Now (3 series)

AR-15, 2012
3D printer, iron, bronze, limestone

Smart Bomb, 2012
3D printer, iron, plastic, bronze

Gas Mask, 2012
3D printer, rubber, plastic

At 5 P.M., the Drog is still missing, and the museum is in the process of entering into a state of panic. With a multimillion-dollar project on the loose in a multibillion-dollar establishment, damage control is the highest priority. We have emergency control for the situation of lost birds, cats, dogs, and squirrels; the problem is that we've never dealt with something that isn't ... living.

I volunteer to stay late with Robby and a handful of other techs, the herd of us heading to the main atrium, where we find Michael Landy handing out headlamps and baseball bats to another handful of preparators and techs. I approach him caustically.

"A baseball bat, really?"

"Just a precaution. Nothing to be concerned about. My baby *does* have a mind of its own."

"You sure don't seem to be worried."

The Fifth Wall

He raises his eyebrows.

"I mean, this could be the biggest moment of our *lives*," I joke, "—the start of a real war against machines."

Michael Landy leans in close. "Isn't that the ultimate goal?" he whispers. "Reaching the point where the machine can think and act on its own. You're right—I'm secretly thrilled."

Sighing, I accept a headlamp and baseball bat and walk over to Robby, who's pacing around the far side of the atrium.

"He's going all Dr. Frankenstein on us," I say.

Robby, with pursed lips, holds up a finger and shakes his head. He's in the middle of a thought.

A tech I recognize approaches me. "I heard it went into the women's bathroom and scared the shit out of some lady," he says.

A girl wearing a camouflage sweatshirt turns around. "I heard it made a little boy cry."

I imagine myself peeing while the headless Drog peers under the stall and I shiver. I then stare at the girl's sweatshirt, and then up at her face.

There is something very peculiar about this whole scenario.

Robby stops pacing and charges towards the center of the room. He quickly breaks us into groups and assigns us specific collections and areas. He then hands each group a walkie-talkie.

"Testing, testing," I say with an English accent into the mic. Robby gives me *the look*. He motions for Michael Landy, who approaches the front of the mob, smacking a baseball bat into his palm in slow, calculated movements. I roll my eyes at this ridiculous gesture. The whole evening's becoming entirely absurd.

"Remember folks—this is a project spent years in the making... it's worth millions of dollars. Be cautious, be careful, be *wise*. It's programmed to be able to somewhat 'feel' when anyone's in its near vicinity, so be aware that you're trying to find something that knows you're there. It's not like chasing a Furby or anything. This is a highly intelligent creature."

Robby's eyes look like they've been swallowed by his face. I feel for the man—this is not something he has room to deal with right now.

For the effect, I clasp the headlamp to my forehead with a loud snap. "Onward!" I shout, holding up the bat. My group follows behind me, laughing.

The empty halls echo with footsteps as we search the massive building for clues and signs. We tiptoe from room to room, peering around sculptures, underneath desks, taking dares to enter first into bathrooms, storage closets, dead-ended galleries. The whole thing feels increasingly eerie, like we're on the set of some indie horror film.

At 5:40, the walkie-talkie spurts with a throaty, crackling voice. The Drog's been spotted turning a corner on the fifth floor. Robby shouts directions for certain groups to take the stairwells, and others to head up directly to the floor. My group takes Stairwell B. We wait impatiently for almost an hour.

"You think there'd be some sort of off button—an emergency abort code."

"This asshole might just be trying to make a statement."

"You mean like a performance piece?"

"Wouldn't he want more of an audience for that?"

"Hi everyone—you're on *Candid Camera!*"

The walkie-talkie spurts, checking in. No sign of the Drog yet—just a sculpture tilted on its wrong axis. Robby curses through the static.

After another hour and a half of different positions and maneuverings, and with two more potential Drog sightings, but no leads, Robby shouts that he needs a smoke, and for us to get our acts together with some fresh air—we aren't leaving tonight without finding the damn thing.

I sigh and descend the steps out to a side exit into the fresh, open air. The night outside is clear and crisp, the stars bright and pulsating. An automatic light turns on, partially blinding me, causing me to turn around swiftly towards the street—and *smack.*

"Sheila?"

My heart stops. I look up through the pulsating red, black, and orange blobs at the person before me—tall and overshadowing—his light brown hair now thinner, cut shorter, more kempt, ruffling in the breeze. Body a little meatier, thicker neck, a stance like a teenager unused to his size; hidden beneath the skin.

Adam's eyes widen, but quickly settle. He takes a drag from his cigarette; I watch smoke billow out from his pucker-pencil-lips. "Well, if it isn't Sheila B. Ackerman."

He nods at me like this is a normal occurrence, like this meeting is somehow inevitably expected. After inhaling once more, he chucks his cigarette on the sidewalk.

"What are you doing here?" he asks, stumbling a bit.

"I work here."

He smiles. It kills me. It feels like I'm being stabbed.

"I thought you were in New York?" he says.

"I was," I nod. "What are you doing here?"

"Ah, I was just—," he points in the direction behind him, "at a horrible bar with horrible people discussing horrible films. It was a fabulous time, really."

I immediately form an image in my brain: the two of us intertwined in complex contortions, our bodies morphing into pornographic abstraction.

I nod, smiling.

"Though the question really is, what are *you* doing here?" He points to the bat in my hand and then to the headlamp.

I laugh at its ridiculousness. "I'm on a mission to find an escaped automaton in the form of a dog without a head."

"*What?*" Adam's eyes widen. He starts cracking up. "You've gotta be fucking kidding me."

I explain to him the situation. I've never seen him more excited. He says he's teaching a make-up seminar tomorrow morning, but begs me to let him help. This is just the kind of trouble he was looking for tonight. Plus it's about time we reconnected. I stare at him, feeling my cells dissipate, scatter, and congeal onto the sidewalk. I have a weird urge to touch him to make sure he's really there.

I lead him back inside and we convene into our groups. Adam pulls out a sizable flask and passes it around. I gulp the burning whiskey down like water.

In an hour, our group is smashed. We stumble through the dark halls, bumping into edges of display cases, giggling and screeching, running and sliding in our socks on the slippery floor. On and off we hear Michael Landy's voice through the walkie-talkie, but no one can piece together what he's saying—each time it sounds like he's continuing reciting some sort of script. The entire time I observe Adam closely, out of the corner of my eye, still baffled at his presence, the timing, the whole situation at hand. Soon Robby gives up and tells us all to go home. A bunch of the volunteers had fled at the break, and the Drog is still nowhere to be found. Apparently the security guard watching the cameras had, cliché-ly, fallen asleep at his desk. Perhaps it escaped through one of the Emergency Exits and is now loose in the city—*who the fuck cares*! Robby throws up his arms, eying Adam curiously as he departs the building with a flamboyant wave.

But where is Michael Landy? It seems no one's physically seen him since the start of the evening. I collect the walkie-talkies in a cardboard box in the atrium while Adam smokes outside, and wait around for a couple of minutes, but the artist never appears.

[EXT. -]

Adam drives us in his truck to a bar near his apartment in the Tenderloin, a part of town I rarely visit. It's like entering into a David Lynch film—the streets filled with ghastly, writhing bodies ready to attack at any moment. Trash and needles and excrement everywhere. An emaciated mammal will try to sell you a cell phone, and then offer you heroin instead. What is it with me lately, and men with trucks?

[INT. -]

"You're doing *what* now?" Adam chokes on a handful of Goldfish crackers from a glass serving dish he'd snatched from the bar. This bar is dark and dusty with a Los Angeles vibe—filled with small crowded tables with white tablecloths and lit by fluorescent lights. He takes a shot of whiskey and sips a PBR.

"I hired a contractor and we're taking apart the house from the inside out. Well, he's mostly doing it. I helped a little bit in the beginning."

Adam stares at me wide-eyed, shaking his head. "I—I don't even know what to say."

"Oh, and I'm filming it, too. I have a camera set up to a software that records and archives it on my MacBook."

I sip my gin and tonic and we both suddenly crack up. We mimic each other's hiccuping laughter, alcohol spurting from our lips.

"I know you're probably thinking I'm out of my fucking mind."

Adam smooths back his hair in a grand gesture and shakes his head. "No, not at all. I mean, we're all crazy, aren't we? But to different degrees. It's all based on our balance between the internal and the external."

I consider this for a moment.

"But no, I think you're fucking brilliant," he says.

I watch his undulating mouth, the washing down of Goldfish with a slug of PBR, an Adam's apple rise and deplete. I don't think I've ever actually seen him eat. He lights up a cigarette. Apparently this is one of the last bars in the city where you can smoke. He offers me one, but I decline. I've oddly never felt the desire.

"So let me just get this straight." Adam blows a gust of smoke away from me.

"You somehow got permission to obliterate your house."

I nod, though technically my dad and brother have no idea, but I told them I was taking care of it.

"And now you're still in the process of deconstructing it, and you're also *filming* it on some sort of live feed that is also being recorded."

I nod, squeezing more of the lime into my drink.

He scratches his chin, contemplating, then inhales deeply.

"My father," he says, "died of a heart attack when I was nineteen. It was really rough. We had a lot of differences, and I'd just moved out of the house to go to college, but still I wasn't prepared for it. Nobody was. It was a huge fucking mess. I mean, like, *yeah*—how are we supposed to deal with these things, really?"

"Exactly," I slam my hand on the table. "We're not actually *prepared* for death. We live in a world that's completely shocked by death—not the brutal deaths we see constantly in movies and on TV, but real, *actual* death. What happens after the fatal moment."

"We stood around a casket and participated in a ritual we didn't even understand. A stranger read scripture and paraphrased my father's obituary in the fucking present tense."

"An ancient woman led us to a small vista behind her horse barn that looked out onto a neighbor's yard. The yard was frozen and covered with snow, and the ashes just plopped down into the snow and sat there—no wind or anything to carry them away into the 'great yonder.' Just a pile of wet ashes and an eighty-year-old woman standing behind us coughing up a storm of phlegm."

"Jesus." Adam signals for another round. "Where's the romance?"

I slurp the remains of my drink. "You know I originally

wanted to just blow it up—demolish the whole fucking property and just settle it at that. But then some layer of reality resolved and forced me to work within society's structured flows. The deconstruction at first was a kind of settling, but now it's become much more compelling—the intention that goes into every dismantled piece. It's not just a one-time decision, but days, hours, minutes of calculated steps. To watch the ripping out of a floorboard scuffed from our shoes, the walls with our pencil marks—the crevices where Caleb and I had written our names. I'm realizing that to truly insult a structure is to break it down. Piece by piece, nail by nail."

"Well, it's art." Adam lights another cigarette.

I shake my head in protest. The performance wasn't even mine to begin with. I walked in the door, and there she was. It's like the timing was set, the staging planned. The greatest performance of all: a witnessed coincidence. My mother, the artist supreme.

"I see it as more of a life experiment," I say. "Transcending the act—merely using film as a way of archiving; I don't intend to *show* this anywhere."

"Oh you're so full of your own shit, and you know it." His smoke circles the booth, entering my lungs, collecting in my pores.

"I mean, how I think about it is this—think of how we store information in computers. When you destroy a computer, all your information is lost—rather, your computer loses its memory. This is how I think about the house."

"Well, *obviously*, Sheila, but your analogy's a little outdated, considering, for instance, cloud backup storage, and the unseen framework that technology instills...the house, yes, will disappear, but the contents inside of it will live on invisibly, in you."

"And in the video," I add.

"Right, of course. Documentation as memory. The camera is the ultimate romantic invention."

I think of all the technology being installed for *The Last Art*—screens projecting 3D interfaces of computed data of city structures mirroring coral reef patterns, the inner workings of the Internet resembling Dark Matter and the biological structure of the brain. All of it raw data translated to moving colored lines, shifting like ghosts in a digitalized non-place. The display of "Smart Art" weaponry—the world's first laser-guided bomb, plus current laser and satellite-guided bombs. A GPS-ed bomb. A 3D-printed AR-15. Artificial hearts and lean slabs of beef growing in Petri dishes. A film about the world's first artificial organism. A whole room filled with thousands of mounted smart phones displaying viral YouTube videos, Instagram and Facebook posts, text and picture messages... everything is "happening" now in a way that feels self-generating, and yet it's all actually outside of us, information circling around us at a rate faster than time, producing total disorientation, amnesia, panic. We talk about the world as if we have a clear concept of what it is—its satellite image as familiar to us as a photograph of our friends, but we actually have no fucking clue. Technology's been able to make the Earth feel completely known. One great big illusion we've all grown accustomed to.

"Your family has no idea, do they?" Adam stares inquisitively at me.

I down his shot of whiskey in response.

"You're a fucking terrorist, is what you are."

We both burst out laughing again. I cough from all the smoke, hiccuping some half-digested Goldfish—Adam scoots up his chair and pats me on the back, but it's no use—I have a case of the giggles.

"I'm a terrorist!" I throw my arms into the air and nearly fall over laughing. I can feel the energy of Adam's body, both its familiarity and foreignness penetrating my senses. There is a potency to the air—a heightened energy I feel within my

The Fifth Wall

bones. The world feels open to endless possibilities, the present unfixed and pulsating throughout the room.

This bar, our table, the lighting and garish white tablecloths—as if the backdrop to our lives from the beginning of time.

How easily our brains allow us to become comfortable.

And it hits me with incredible force. The realization that up until my mother's suicide, I'd felt a great disenchantment with the world. It was something I'd always felt since childhood—this life with a filter. The only time I'd experienced it lifting was on September 11th in 2001, when both fantasy and terror entered the world as we watched, on repeat, the towers explode and crumble to the ground. Isn't that when I started making art?

The honest truth is that, as the house dismantles, I feel more alive. Veins of power burst within the falling walls.

Fuck, I *am* a terrorist.

Adam's eyes sparkle. He grabs me by the jaw and kisses me violently. Chapped lips firm and aggressive, the massaging of a bitter, smoky tongue.

I topple onto him.

"You're so fucking *sexy.*" He grabs me at the waist and pulls me closer, sucks harder at my mouth.

I obey his actions through harsh, heavy breaths, my nerves galactic and spiraling with adrenaline.

Before I know it we're stumbling outside and heading towards his apartment, the moon a bright white orifice blazing from the face of a treacherous sky.

It happens while we're having sex. *The Lack*—no longer restricted to the instance with the axe. I come out of it as he's exploding into me, the both of us shrieking bloody murder.

It takes me a few moments to realize what's happened, to register the ruffled sheets, the smoky air, the heaving mass above me.

Adam collapses beside me, moaning with delight. He pulls me close to him. He says he was watching my face the entire time—that as I was reaching my peak, my expression broke out into the most horrifying contortion he'd ever seen. I ask him what happened then? He looks at me slightly disappointed. You mean you don't remember? He asks. I say I was just really caught up in it—that it's all kind of a blur. He laughs, saying that that's when I started screaming. I was *shrieking*, like seriously, at the very top of my lungs. And it freaked him out so much in such a profound way that he began having an orgasm himself! He says I was screaming out of what—no joke—looked like a crucifixion-fetishist must look like during the nailing—this type of excruciating, masochistic arousal—and that he began shouting, too, because he was fantastically shooting into me while also at the same time trying to pull out from me because he'd forgotten to put on a condom.

"Fuck," I say.

"Are you not on the pill, baby?" He strokes my arm.

I am on the pill. But had I been remembering to take it? My mother, even as a nurse, had been totally against it. She thought it a terrifying experiment to try to change the course of evolution. That pumping your body full of hormones was like absorbing radiation—it worked scientifically on some levels, but left your body fending for itself without its own source of protection. But condoms feel awful, and I never trust myself always to use them.

"Don't worry—it's all good." I stroke his mess of dandruffy curls.

The strewn pile of my clothes buzzes on the hardwood, its vibrations permeating the structure of the room, the bed frame, our trembling bodies. Déjà vu hits me like a whirlwind, my heartbeat pacing to the floor's quiet rumble.

A real artist is someone who acts, Adam had said to me at some point during the night. *Who interrogates, who coerces, who takes radical risks.* I close my eyes and focus inward, trying to center myself amidst the relentless chaos.

Is this what it feels like, then—to be fully consumed? Possessed by internal forces? Engulfed by fantasy?

My phone continues to buzz on the floor. I stare at the ceiling, feeling the vibrations of its ringing in the sweat-soaked bed, my exhausted body.

I let it ring.

In my dream, it's dark outside—so dark it feels thick as acrylic with blackness. Adam and I roam long, narrow hallways in a building that appears to be a combination of the architecture of SFMoMA, Adam's apartment, my mother's house, and Mal's pizzeria. I hear a loud growling noise and turn towards a cavernous hall of pitch-black, seeming to call out to me from the depths of its interior. I spin back around to find Adam, but he's gone. A hollow fills my stomach. I bolt down the dark hallway, flailing my arms and legs, and come upon a clearing—grassy, a hill—a very steep hill, with fog circling all around it. In front of me appears Maddie, Jesse's dog, the senior citizen, pattering around, looking lost. I walk over to pet her, bending down and nuzzling my face into hers. I feel a lot of comfort. Warmth. Suddenly the hill drops and gets very, very steep and high—almost vertical, like the peak of a mountain—as if being pulled down by a force, nearly causing us to fall. Maddie becomes very large, like a horse, and flailing—her eyes, burning red, become glazed over with white. She begins growling, producing devilish noises, spurting in a language I can't seem to understand. I gasp, and watch as Maddie's face disappears, her body altering to the technological nature of the Drog, as it looms over me, faceless and writhing with various interworking mechanisms and parts. I know that there is evil here. This world I've entered into is wholly unsafe. I feel tremendous pain, guilt, and loss, as we are pulled down into the mountainous abyss.

Adam Black (b. 1979)
The Terrorist, 2013
Fresh semen splattered inside Sheila B. Ackerman

The next morning, the Walgreens pharmacist hands me a thin cardboard package containing two small white pills you release by popping them through a sleek foil barrier. She observes my tired face—messy hair, smudged mascara—frowning.

"Do you have any questions?" she asks.

I shake my head and pay the outrageous forty dollars for the Plan B. I'd taken it a few times in college after a few nebulous evenings involving my friend Victor's famous punch laced with pure MDMA.

A muted TV flashes the news; a scrolling news line reads CAL-IFORNIA EARTHQUAKES EXCEED RECORD ANNUAL NUMBER. A sense of uncertainly fills me. Have they been happening with my no longer feeling them?

My phone buzzes in my pocket. Texts I haven't even looked at from last night. I scroll through them while heading to the exit of the store. Jesse wondering where I am. A fantasy scenario of what he wants to do to me. I browse over it without really reading it, my brain right now lacking the room for that kind of play. A message from Caleb—long, fucking *so* long—a text that takes what feels like a full minute to scroll back to its beginning:

CALEB
Last night during ceremony I felt the full weight of the earth.
I broke through the body mold. The air became my body, the

73

plants my skin, the dirt my blood. It had been raining in the jungle for days up until last night. At first I felt the nourishment of the plants—the water seeping through my being, down to my roots and soil—so beautiful and natural and pure. But then I started to drown. I felt like I was being suffocated, the water now too much water. I felt the earth cry out, I felt its reactive body. The unnatural weather patterns, the diseases, the way the earth is responding to industrialization, global-ization, fighting to survive! The world is a dying organism, Sheila. A dying organism with a toxic mass inside. The feeling was so strong that my body started to physically shake, and waves of terrible sadness rippled through me. I understood what Mom must have been feeling . . . this terrible weight, this body knowing of its end, the pain it was already enduring, and what it was preparing to endure. The Shaman came and sat in front of me. He sang deep, throaty noises at me while I tried desperately not to scream. The weight was so heavy, Sheils. She felt so trapped. She couldn't bear to let it take her like that. And then at some point a memory flooded into me which I hadn't remembered in years but which was of mom carrying me up the stairs as a little boy and her spooning me until I fell asleep. I had totally forgotten about it. I saw how u and I, when we were really young, brought so much life into Mom and Dad, how they loved to show us new

A finger taps me on the shoulder, and I stop reading the message. A tired man pushes past me into the Walgreens. I can't fucking take this right now, Caleb. I shove my phone back in my pocket, pop the first pill in my dry mouth and swallow, and head down the windy street towards home.

The Mission reeks of urine and sizzling maize pupusas. The overcast sky casts a stale, charcoal glow. I pass by a weather-worn tent sheltering a sleeping body exuding an overwhelming stench of filth and decay. A woman in stilettos clicks by me

The Fifth Wall

rapidly, yelling into an earpiece; a man holds out his cell phone in front of his face, conducting some sort of interview. A crying woman muttering to herself stops and asks me for fifty cents; she thrusts a dirty cup into my face and I push her away—not now, not *today*, for Christ's sake. A tremendous nausea comes over me. Clutching my stomach, I move along the streets trying to maintain an inner balance so I don't hurl this pill up and have to spend another forty bucks. This whole lost city's filled with people talking to themselves; even the young entrepreneurs look totally schizophrenic. A body enters through an open glass door a few businesses down from me, and I head for the building—anything to just get off the street.

Inside is a small, heated waiting room. A young receptionist sits at a desk lit by dim track lighting, across from her two chairs framing a table with an insulated spouted thermos, tiny paper cups, and a pile of health and wellness magazines. A sign on the wall reads WELCOME TO A COMMUNITY ACUPUNCTURE CLINIC. PLEASE SPEAK WITH A WHISPER, AND HELP YOUR-SELF TO SOME TEA. The young receptionist looks up at me and smiles wide. She tiptoes out from behind the desk.

"Thank *God* you're here," she whispers to me. "I've had to pee like crazy for the past *hour*." She rushes to lock the door behind me and asks me to keep an eye on a woman, whom she points to, behind a shadowed room divider. I peer behind the divider and spot a woman, alone, sitting up on one of the four sheet-lined recliner chairs, eyes closed, breathing heavily, with a massive protruding stomach. Tiny acupuncture needles poke out from her wrists, shoulders, head, and ankles; her hands grasp beneath her enormous swollen belly. "She was feeling a little light-headed and dizzy earlier," the receptionist says. "I just didn't want to leave her alone!" She shuffles towards the back to the bathroom. Beads of sweat drip from the pregnant woman's brow, her lips swollen, parted loosely, her body at the edge of her seat, mind turned inwards as if she's listening to something communicating from inside. I stand gaping in front of her, feeling like both a stranger and a ghost in this bizarre situation of great intimacy, wrongly witnessing some sort of private moment mistakenly handed to me—too symbolic to possibly exist. Soft sounds emanate from an adjacent room; shadows through the screened door reveal an acupuncturist helping another patient. The woman inhales and exhales with great, palpable force, her body brimming to its edges with vitality. I feel an energy pulsing through her so familiar and yet so foreign—this body carrying this great, living weight. The biology in my body twisting and turning, feeling her splitting cells.

The receptionist returns, thanking me, and rushes to unlock the door. I bolt out of it, nearly tripping on the sidewalk, running at full speed.

My mother would carry us up the stairs, one by one, and tuck us into our beds. She'd lay with each one of us until we fell asleep. Was it growing inside her then? This great toxic particle blooming in her brain as she recited *Goodnight Moon* from memory, tucked wisps of hair behind my ears? Oh Caleb, why do you have to be so fucking *understanding*? She *couldn't bear to let it take her like that*—but she *could* bear to leave us this way? If only you knew! Had the darkness taken over her motor skills, worked its icy tentacles into her frontal cortex, disturbing her whatever-it-is that processes *common fucking decency*, my God! If *we* only knew—there is so much we could have done! The Earth is dying from our selfishness—but what about me? New research shows cancer possibly lurking in our DNA—right now a tumor could be growing inside me at a microscopic rate. What's to stop it? Perhaps we all have this darkness living inside of us—this growing *lack* starting from the day we are born, invisible and waiting for the right moment, living alongside of us as we move and fuck and speak.

The film furrows and chafes; black and white lines zigzagging along the color image. My dad asks her a question and she

The Fifth Wall

begins to answer it. He zooms in until her face fills the screen. Focusing in, the curves of her face become craters, valleys and mountains. Her face becomes a map. The TV screen's a mirror. All cameras have a coercive nature—a natural quality of the camera is to be obscene. Penetrating angles from all angles from every direction, every space unseen. Long shot, wide shot, medium shot, close-up; dolly, tracking, pan, tilt, zoom. The closest resemblance to *pure consciousness*. But I can't for the life of me make out what she fucking says.

A house has eyes all over its body—its whole body is a face. A house watches us, is witness to our lives. Its façade is a wall of protection, an armor that will last much longer than us. You can bolt the locks, seal the windows, set up a complex security system to prevent intrusion—and yet, like in a horror film, the killer always gets inside.

A house will shelter you from everything but yourself.

On one of the Handycam tapes I salvaged, labeled *1988*, there is a segment that I don't remember—an instance I couldn't possibly have seen. This is a segment that exists in the middle of two taped events: 1, my brother's baseball game and 2, my third birthday party. The segment enters after twenty seconds of black. The camera flips on and it's a bright summer morning; light reflects off the vertical kitchen windows, creates an encompassing aerial calm blue. A framed print of Warhol's quadrupled John Lennon. A potted aloe plant. A blood-orange mug of steaming coffee. My mother sits at the kitchen table cutting strips of paper. Beside her is a shiny compact metal box. The camera moves slowly towards her, the frame wobbling with each step. It creeps up behind her. Her hair is tied up with a lavender scrunchie. Lower-scalp fuzz. Visible neck birthmark. *And just what are we doing here?* My dad speaks, and my mother jumps with fright, turns and sees the camera, clutches her heart, laughs. *Christ, Danny,* she says, smiling into the camera, *you just can't get enough of that thing, can you?* A toaster pop. A candle. The ticking Kit-Cat clock. *Explain to the camera what you're doing.* My dad's hand appears and strokes her hair. My mother leans into his touch. His hand falls outside of the screen. *I'm making a time capsule,* she says. The camera moves beside her to try and get a glimpse. My mother purses her lips, pushes my dad back playfully. *Come on, Daniel.* The camera turns to face her profile, zooms in so that her face fills the screen. She turns towards us and giggles, her eyes glassy and bright. Her cheeks hibiscus red. *Enough of that, come on.* She turns away to cover the other materials. *Seriously, Daniel,* she tries to sound stern. *For real,* she says, *fucking come on.*

78

At work, as we begin mapping out the Serra installation, there's a heightened energy in the atmosphere, but also the feeling of imminent catastrophe—the whole crew together in one space amped up in preparation for Richard Serra's multimillion-dollar *Band*—measuring and marking the concrete ground of the lower atrium, bringing in the forklifts, gantries, and cranes, setting up winches, skids, and slings. Robby's more anxious than I've ever seen him—running around with a headset and his shirt untucked, triple-checking everyone's status and station—*yes, I will be standing right over by the doors, yes, I will be overseeing piece number three.* Rushing bodies, leg spasms, the rumbling of heavy machines—anticipation is everywhere.

In the past two days, there have been signs of the Drog, but still no discovery. A tiny piece of its machinery was found by the Rachel Whiteread sculpture. A security cam caught it walking slowly through the third floor media room, but somehow it immediately disappeared. A few times I've run briefly into Michael Landy, appearing more and more haggard looking since the missing of his Drog, as if he hasn't even left the museum since. There's rumors of him crouching in corners, whispering into the walkie-talkie, his glasses lopsided, his hair spiked up in all directions, his black t-shirt toothpaste-stained and tearing.

"Now, Brandon—drive the crane over about twenty meters to the right corner of the atrium, and we'll unload there. *Sheila Ackerman*, go stand there and wait for him."

"Feet, Robby, feet. Speak American."

Robby lowers his megaphone and rolls his eyes. He stands on a raised platform in the middle of the museum's garage. Both barn doors are propped ajar to reveal four rear-facing trucks open and displaying guts of dismantled pieces of *Band* like dead branches, unmagnificent without the tree. We help unload them using cranes and the steady hands of trained technicians, the majority of whom are most likely hungover, subsisting on stale bagels and endless coffee refills. Orange cones lead from the garage to an opening in the makeshift wall of the lower atrium, where the massive sculpture will be installed.

"Sheila, earth to *Sheila*."

I am a human Transformer. Watch me carry almost one ton of steel in my hands.

The technician lifts Piece #3, the lower half of an S-shape. It's golden brown and as thick as the length of an index finger. The curve of the steel is flawless, its weight invisible beneath its flowing simplicity.

"Sheila, what are you waiting for? A full moon? Let's get a move on!"

I feel as if a hand is putting pressure on my chest, holding me back while the room stretches forward, expands into a separate, flat dimension. My awareness of the room changes. The scene splits up.

A crane. A helmet. A pivot. A truck. The room becomes filled with objects.

I start to actually look at them. They are foreign, unfamiliar. I see a room filled with things, but it's not just a room anymore. A platform. A steering wheel. A concrete ground.

Agile metalwork, corrugated steel. They pop out of the room, these foreign entities, as if someone has cut and pasted them, a duplicate world on top of the original. A two-dimensional space.

I lift my arm to touch them. Perhaps if I feel them, they'll become real.

"*What the hell is she doing?*"

And the air feels strange. It feels as if something is missing, but everything's too vague to tell, or really be sure. There's a connection and disconnection all at once. I am here, but not here.

The Fifth Wall

"Am I speaking English, Sheila, or have I become a fucking mute? *Get out of the way of the crane.*"

A blinding white flash.

The bike falls on top of me. Cold steel smashes against my skin. I throw the bike off of me; it hits the floor with a stiff thud. I reach out to touch her head. There is no way I cannot look.

"*STOP, STOP!*"

My mother faces away from me; I know it's her and yet I have to see. I have to see. The fly is buzzing; the sound is getting louder and louder. I need to see.

Someone is squeezing my arm. A burning. A sharpness. And then a flood of cold.

"Fuck!" I scream. "What the fuck!"

Someone is pouring water over me. I cover my face with frantic gestures, confused at what has happened, at what is going on.

"Sheila? Can you hear me?"

A crowd circles around me in the museum's garage. I hear Robby in the background panicking over the sculpture; one of the curator's kids shrieks that he wants a banana. Robby hovers over me, eyes wide and straining. I blink just to make sure it's real. "What just happened?" I hear myself saying. "What is this?" I feel myself shaking. I realize I'm lying in the middle of the atrium. Robby touches the back of his hand to my forehead. It feels cool, and light, and smooth, and I want it off me this *very* instant.

"Sheila, are you okay?"

"I'm *fine*," I say, and hurl myself off the ground, push through the crowd. I make no eye contact, allow no indication of hesitancy, in fear I might see her face. In fear that at any moment, if I stop for just a second, I'll collapse.

I walk out of Robby's office and up the atrium staircase to a hallway just off the main lobby where the restrooms are. I push open the door with unusual force; it accelerates into the doorstop, clangs and reverberates across the floor. Two receptionists look towards me, their palms open and raised.

I shrug my shoulders and walk with my head down out through the revolving glass elliptical into an open and less concentrated light.

I'd sat in Robby's office for a long time, my head buried in my lap, unsure of what to say or how to say it. He asked me to explain what happened a series of times. *I remember standing there and watching the crane start to move and thinking, "I'm going to walk over there now," and then feeling water splashing all over me.* He asked me to repeat it again and again, but that's all I could really come up with. *There's something lurking inside of me that I don't recognize,* I finally shouted at him. *A presence I have never felt before. I think I might be dying.*

He told me that I'd better take some time off to recuperate and revitalize. That there are some things in life that, no matter how strong we are or think we are, just need time. I protested dramatically, but he said it was an order. I'd slammed the door in his face, shrieking that I needed a shot.

Try to calm down. I decide to walk back to my apartment. Nothing is ever *that* serious. The Lack probably has a simple explanation. I Google the symptoms on my phone again. A new possibility turns up: PTSD. PTSD, or a food allergy. This website recommends an elimination diet. Another website says it's all due to low cortisol levels. Another website says it's the body responding to an alien invasion.

Oh, if only it were that simple.

At home, I swab the inside of my mouth with a Q-tip and seal it inside a plastic bag. I place the plastic bag, along with a check for one hundred dollars, in a cardboard box addressed to a small facility in Germany, who will email me in a week of their receiving it with the results. I'd run into Mal just as she was leaving for Harbin Hotsprings, and had remembered her talking about this kit the other week. It turned out she had an extra one from some health expo—that this company is known for their honest procedures, their holistic background, their precise attention to detail. The agreement promises the email will contain every possible deficiency in my body, every piece of microscopic matter that my body has ever lacked. My DNA reduced to names and percentages on an intricately ordered list.

Across the street from my apartment is the San Francisco School for Blind Children. This afternoon an instructor is leading a group of a half-dozen five-year-olds in a single file line, attempting to introduce them to a world that exists unseen. I watch them from the window—small, fragile, bouncing bodies smile with grasping hands extending, reaching up, bending down, touching everything. One little boy meows, pretending he's a cat. To think a blind child can have a sense of humor! The ambling pack mimics him, laughing. The instructor tries to calm them down, allows herself to laugh for a moment, and then quickly becomes stern. *Now what is to your right?* She is asking. *What is to your left?* Up, down, touch the ground. *Everywhere is really nowhere, children. We're all lost and blind, even with two eyes that see.*

We now inhabit the realm of the infraluminic, I hear Michael Landy's voice, staticky through a walkie-talkie. *The limits of speed have been reached—except for computing speed, of course. It's not the end of human history, but the end of a historical regime. History is happening now, synchronized to world time, live from this very moment . . .*

Since Mal took her car, I borrow her bike and ride towards BART. I don't want to think right now, I just need to *move.* Twenty minutes underground and I'm rolling up just as Jesse's removing the flooring material—almost down to the last remaining floor joists that form its basic foundation. The house is almost gone. His face lights up when he sees me. I drag him over to his truck and push him inside, where we fuck fervently in the grimy back seat. He loves every second of it. I feel like crying.

I have this vision while I'm riding my bike. It happens mostly when gliding down hills at night, my feet locked into place, gravity dictating speed. What happens is I'll be coasting and suddenly I'll see a transparent, imaginary world on top of the real world. It will be like I am both myself and seeing myself at the same time. And what happens is first something falls off—it's not in the same order every time.

But let's say that this time, first my left handle bar falls off, and then my left pedal. And then the right. Then it's suddenly the back wheel. I am gliding and suddenly my bike is falling apart right beneath me, and yet I do not fall. Then go the gears, and the brakes, the seat, and the other handle bar. The frame scours the pavement, drags jaggedly without sound. Off goes the stem that held up the handlebars, and then the front wheel.

Then everything disappears.

I'm trying to know a distance. In grad school, one assignment was to walk everywhere—to understand the feeling of from *here* to *there*. The whole class was based on making maps. The idea was that an artist is never here nor there, their work is never this nor that. There's no fixed agenda, no endpoint, no solution. Artists work as a means of exploring the relationships between things.

One guy in my class fastened a fifty-pound anchor to his leg; for a week, he literally dragged the thing everywhere. He looked idiotic, but the idea was legitimate. He wanted to feel time.

I, shockingly, recorded everywhere I went. But there was a catch—I attached a digital camcorder to my backpack. Instead of a forward movement, the distance became a retreat. I literally put eyes in the back of my head. The hindrance of not seeing created a tension. The effect was like facing the opposite direction on a train—movement is reversed: it is the landscape that moves away.

At TC 96:52:15.54, in slow motion, my body bends at the waist, knees, and ankles, arms reaching, fingers spreading, hands blooming. I grasp the heavy tool, my muscles tightening—as I lift it towards my right shoulder, raise it higher and higher, my left foot stepping forward, and then my right, my left, my right, until it's a rapid succession of leg muscles straining, a gorgeous pattern of swift, flawless movement. I don't know where I acquired such steadfast legs—so purposeful, so resolute. From behind, I can feel my eyes piercing like living candles, like a vivid reflection, on fire. I am heaving the axe into the sheathing—my pixelated wrists revolving in their sockets in an action of desperate *BOOM*, a splatter of fibers—a heaving, strenuous pull. I feel the power of exhilaration, of scattering, multiplying cells. The axe flails out, leaving the house framing my erratic, violent body. Screen distortion for a moment before a large, incoming tan hand grabs my wrist and constricts.

I pause the video.

What if it were Adam?

That night Adam and I meet at a small local brewery where he knows the bartender and we toast to the end of his spring semester teaching over incredibly rich, ten percent barley wines. Around us bodies press up against other bodies, breathing heat into one another, filling the air with a moist density. The lighting is dim, the only luminescence projected from the bar's overhead lights onto a colorful wall lined with at least twenty different taps, the rest of the room shallow and thin, black walls forming a rectangular aperture filled with standing tables, a jukebox, obscured bar art, the faceless clenching together in dark spaces. An illuminated Exit sign burns red above the back door. Here, voices fuse together into hollow echoes; noise is one collective mass. Body odor sticks to surfaces, insulates the collective muddle brazen with displaced energy, weary from daylight. The young living-dead.

This, here, is the end of the world. I glance around the room. This *must* be where it ends.

"I peed in a jar earlier," I tell him. "Dustin was shaving or something and I couldn't hold it so I just ran into the kitchen and grabbed one of Mal's empty sprouting jars and took it back into my room and just peed in it."

Adam bursts out laughing. "Not to sound creepy, but I really wish I'd been there to witness that." His cool, dry hand touches my waist.

"It was a really bizarre feeling. It was like I re-remembered how it felt to be an animal. Like—*oh*, right, I am *also* something that has to perform certain bodily functions that apparently can't always bow to cultural etiquette. Here I am squatting in my bedroom where I do many other private things that are *not* peeing, but yet this feels completely ridiculous because when I look at this jar, I'm looking at something that holds a product I can consume."

"I once tried to piss in a car on a road trip." Adam's hand moves up and down my waist. "I was in the passenger seat of my buddy's car. We were driving east for Christmas, and it was really late, and cold—all I remember is this really uncomfortable moment of having my dick pressed into a stale coffee cup."

I laugh.

"But I just couldn't do it. I had to go so badly that I thought I was going to piss my pants. But even then, I don't know—for some reason it felt wrong." He brushes a piece of hair behind my ear. "I felt like a woman—I couldn't go because of the *ambiance*."

I push him playfully and he laughs, coughs deeply, takes a sip of barley wine.

"So what happened?" I ask. "Did you pee or didn't you pee?"

"We pulled over to the side of the road. Apparently I'd rather piss in the freezing cold pitch-black."

"You were so far gone from your animal spirit that your body would rather *implode* than release its toxins in an unfamiliar space."

"Right—a typical closet case."

We both giggle, allowing some of my tension to release. I tell him how I often feel like a slave to my bodily functions, and he responds that he considers defecating just as he considers eating and sleeping—as diseases. Anything that takes you away from the real work to be done. I consider this while watching him slug down the last of the barley wine and order an IPA from the menu, his hands jittery with nicotine cravings. He asks me for an update on the Drog, and I tell him that we've found nothing yet, but also that Michael Landy seems to be falling off the wagon. He walks around speaking into a walkie-talkie to no one, taking on some sort of psychotic role that still feels oddly staged, and yet I haven't seen him break the mold, nor talked to him directly for more than thirty seconds. I don't mention the Serra sculpture, or my temporary dismissal—details entirely unnecessary for him to know. Nor do I mention how the world has taken on a nightmarish quality—how it feels like an uncanny layer of reality has inserted itself directly over the present one, as I watch myself play out a role I designed for myself the second I saw my mother pull the trigger.

At some point our conversation turns to installation art.

"These days I feel like installation art is too aware of itself," says Adam. "It's like, you go into a museum and immediately there's a written blurb about the exhibition, the artist, and the history behind the artist's work. You read some condensed version of one person's analysis and suddenly you're looking at the art with a biased eye. And if you choose not to read the blurbs, you're still thrown into a realm of artifice. You walk in a room designed to display—poisoned already by even the *existence* of the blurbs, not to mention the other museum visitors obstructing your total absorption."

I nod, sipping from his beer. "That's pretty much the catch-22 of the museum space."

"So, ideally," Adam continues, "there's a barrier between art and entertainment, and everyday life going on outside of that—installation art is then supposed to break that barrier by re-introducing a subjective experience back into art. It invites the viewer to survey and evaluate, to invoke a personal experience . . . a *feeling*. But now there's too much of a filter."

"So you think art should be returning to a notion of involvement—not just something to look at or absorb from a distance?"

"Fucking exactly. We've become solely spectators of art. High art's become so conditioned to white walls that even our awareness of its flaws no longer provides any useful conflict. And performance art's turned into this whole façade of culture—I mean, it's all about *re*performance now. What's the fucking point without the context?"

"We need another Fluxus movement. Another Yoko Ono, another Carolee Schneemann, another Valie Export in some fucking shocking Action Pants. Let's bring them all back from the dead!"

"How about a Sheila B. Ackerman?" Adam eyes me slyly.

I smile, and order the same beer from the bartender. "Well, the house will be gone by tomorrow."

"Then we have *two* reasons to celebrate tonight!"

"Yes, to the erasure of history, childhood, suicide, and death."

"To the dismantling of the distinction between art and life."

"And . . . to this beer." I burst out laughing.

"Yes, of course, without this beer we would be terribly boring."

"Without this beer *you* might be terribly boring, but I would still be just as interesting, just maybe . . . sadder."

"All right." We both chuckle. "This toast ended four toasts ago," he says.

We chink glasses and gulp them down, our bodies quickly settling into the night that lies ahead.

At around 2 A.M. we stumble out onto the windy streets of the city, barely able to contain ourselves. It's a Saturday night, so the streets are still crawling with last calls, voices echoing as we pass swiftly by closed doors. The city spins gloriously, my body buzzing from a mixture of alcohol, horniness, and despair. We stagger through the Tenderloin, becoming shadows amongst the crowds of forsaken, soulless bodies, having given up themselves to cravings, lost in the murmuring of millions of past lives, telling and being retold to eternity. I don't know why or how it starts, but all of a sudden Adam's pulling on car handles, testing them to see who's the lucky winner to have forgotten to lock their doors. I follow his lead, laughing at his stupidity, the evening's meaninglessness—how glorious it feels to feel nothing. In the first car we find a painting—some artist's mediocre attempt to mimic Miró. We take it, running from car to car, this huge canvas flapping awkwardly alongside us. I swipe someone's Ray-Bans, which I know I'll never wear. Adam chews some hot cinnamon gum. We set off a car alarm and run. The exhilaration lasts for a little while, until our adrenaline dies down and the alcohol settles. The objects become meaningless, trite, and wholly unnecessary. We leave them in an alley and stagger towards his place.

Sheila B. Ackerman (b. 1984)
Romance (*from graduate thesis: **The Fourth Wall**)*, 2012
Installation and video

The video begins with a three-sided, white-walled gallery space. The camera is centered so that there is one wall in front of you and a wall on either side, suggesting you are possibly in an enclosed room, or a theater. You watch me come out from behind the camera and survey the space. I walk around the perimeter a few times, and then disappear from the frame.

I start to drag in objects until the room becomes filled.

Materials: one (donated) queen size mattress and box spring, floral comforter, high-thread count sheets, multiple pillows, blankets, and shams in lush, muted earthtones of cotton and down. Night stand, record player, long, flowing drapes (also curtain rods, rod holders, nails, screwdrivers—electric and hand-held), strewn book dust-jackets, used tissues, ginger-lemon tea bags, organic dark chocolate, bottles of Malbec, multiple packs of cigarettes.

You watch me assemble a bedroom, a utopian space conjured from both memories and projections of love. A false history composed solely of objects. A fictitious lived-*in*.

I film in order to see a progression from here to there.

We look into the distance in order to be able to see what's right in front of us. Isn't that the point of utopian thought?

But what happens when you project and assemble an architecture of fantasy is the culminating anxiety of its stark falsity, the realness of its inert objects, dead without use.

The walls close in.

Sheila B. Ackerman (b. 1984)
Nightmare, 2013
Images, ideas, emotions, and sensations in the mind during sleep

In my dream, I stand with my back to the camera, facing the room. My posture is straight and stiff, my head cocked slightly to the right. You can't see it, but I'm imagining a desert, a landscape of desolation, death, and dread.

I leave the room for an hour and—fast-forwarding—return with orange paint, packages of sand, rocks, potted cacti, crates and bags of miscellaneous items, a foot-long Home Depot receipt.

I start to fill the room.

Birth control pill-packs. A ventilating mask.

The room grows, swells with cluttered heaviness. Orange paint drips onto the nightstand, the bedspread, the long, flowing drapes. Sand granules collect in piles, inches, feet. Plants sprout from pots, tentacles spreading like lava.

Frame one, frame two, frame two hundred and ten. The walls begin a stark white and become a deep shade of candied orange.

The Fifth Wall

The room takes on a life of its own. A narrative begins to form. Time enters in.

The nightmare begins once it hits that nothing will ever stop changing. That the room will never be—and can never be—*done*. That what exists inside my mind is a lost image that can only be duplicated with objects. That the nature of all art is constant failure.

That memory contains everything.

That the sand will consume us all.

"What's it called?" Adam asks me the next morning.

I ask him what he's talking about.

"The project—the performance. The deconstruction. It has to have a name."

I have no idea, I'm about to say, but then it comes to me instantly.

"The Fifth Wall."

I watch him mouth it silently.

"A space beyond the fourth wall of the theater between audience and stage." I picture my open MacBook, the live image of the almost-empty dirt plot, where so far I've spotted gophers and raccoons and an occasional wild cat. Where I watch the previously recorded footage like I'm an actress on a screen. "An invisible theater where the audience is actually watching themselves."

ACT TWO

There is no route out of the maze.
The maze shifts as you move through it, because it is alive.

PHILIP K. DICK, Valis

The air is dry and dusty, with wind flapping violently through open windows, the sun baking the truck's hot black metal and steel. The highway opens onto a wide expanse of desert sagebrush, barrel cacti, and dogweed. Joshua trees poke their thick, stubby fingers from the parched, reddish earth. Smoke from Adam's cigarette mixes with the desert's fresh, dead scent, the radio crackling as we zoom forward into the vastness of the deep Mojave under a clear blue sky.

Adam holds the wheel with a comfortable carelessness, his body gradually loosening as we penetrate deeper into the desert's landscape. He grew up in this kind of terrain, he tells me, and often feels constricted by the vertical pollution of the city, how it offers much less room for the mind and body to move. I observe a slight drop in his shoulders, a giddiness to his temperament. He takes a swig from a flask and passes it to me. The sharp whiskey burns and soothes. We are driving to a remote location where a group of men will gather to launch objects into the upper atmosphere. Adam met them years ago right before their first launch at a bar in Lancaster, a small town bordering the California side of the Mojave, where he'd stopped during a drive home from his mother's house in Joshua Tree. He'd followed them out to a large expanse and witnessed the initial trials of this bizarre activity. Since then they'd gained a larger following and had created a website with an email list announcing new launch dates and other special local events.

The truck zooms through the lingering breeze of mid morning, just a few hours before the inevitable sweltering heat. We woke up at dawn to get a move on, having spent all of Sunday hungover in bed, watching movies, eating Vietnamese takeout, and fucking in a blur. On the highway, driving itself feels like a practice of amnesia, the speed of the truck along the straight road warping the landscape around us. I take another swig and feel a welcoming haziness, the road seeming to stretch forever towards a fated central point. The service bars on my iPhone vanish as we thrust inside the scene.

We approach a massive stretch of bright crimson ground, as we penetrate acres of blooming poppies basking in the sunlight. A sign reads ANTELOPE VALLEY CALIFORNIA POPPY RESERVE. I reach my arms out of the window as if to touch them, my fingers rippling in the warm air above the red. Adam turns off the road just beyond the reserve—the one reference point in the directions we've been looking for. We drive down a long, bumpy road towards a fading backdrop of snowcapped Sierras.

The plateau is hard and wide, a dusty golden yellow. Slamming the truck door, I drop my sunglasses down from my forehead to shield the sun's oncoming blindness, and am immediately confronted by a large cactus—a tiny brown lizard crawls in-between thin spikes along the massive succulent's protruding arms, raised up to me as if in surrender.

Adam and I approach a group of about a dozen men ranging from a hypothesized age range of late thirties to mid-fifties, all dressed pretty gruffly in dirty jeans and faded button-down tees. Adam's black western boots click satisfyingly on the desert's hardened dirt, his tight black jeans and also tight black v-neck forming a silhouette of himself on the flat, shadeless ground. I roll up my sleeves to catch some light on my pale, freckled skin.

I'd asked Adam what these men could possibly want to shoot up into space. He said he believed it's less about the actual propelled object than the act of propelling it. He remembered lucky baseballs, a few desert rocks, a glass paperweight with some sort of insect carcass embedded inside. He joked about once wanting to shoot up his dissertation, how great it would have felt to watch it blast out of sight and watch hundreds of its teeny tiny remains fall and scatter like ashes over vast distances of desert and light.

Adam, too, has romances about the destruction of things.

A hefty, sunburned man wearing a floppy cowboy hat greets Adam with a masculine one-armed hug and a slap on the back. He introduces himself as Charlie, and welcomes us to the group by popping open two cold cans of Budweiser from a cooler. Sipping the welcome of cold, I follow Charlie to a little station he's created for himself, where he demonstrates how they actually launch the items—a mechanism they developed by using a large helium balloon with a chemical component, which travels up for roughly an hour-and-a-half to two hours until it bursts, the objects reaching anywhere up to about ninety thousand feet. He says he's seen people at NASA who use tracking systems and altitude recorders and tiny little cameras to transmit all the data of the objects for analysis—usually to launch some sort of satellite—like we need any more machines watching our every move.

"You know satellites will outlive us," says Adam.

"*And* all of humanity," I add.

"A ring of machines orbiting the Earth, sending signals to no one."

Charlie brushes dust off of the mechanism. "Well that's a scary thought." He turns it around in his hands. "We boys of the desert like to do it in what I called the *old school way*—just plain shooting regular old objects up into that great and beautiful unknown."

I watch Charlie and a few of the other guys mount what look like metal devices securing their objects to the swollen helium balloons. I identify a silver necklace, an arrowhead, and an empty half-size box of Pringles. Adam downs his beer, crushes it in his hand, and tosses it behind him. He removes two earplugs from his pocket and fits them into his ears.

"Having this kind of power—," he speaks loudly to me now

with the earplugs, "—makes you *have* to believe that creatures like us were sent here to destroy all this." He opens out his arms and breathes in the arid, dusty air. "Our evolution has been fixed since the beginning. The biggest feat for us to realize is that *we're* the enemies."

"On your mark, get set, FIRE!" Charlie and two other men launch the balloons up into the sky. I shove my fingers in my ears to block out the noise. For a split second my head feels swallowed by a deep sound, like being plunged under water. The ground rumbles beneath us. The objects shoot up with tremendous force. Baritone voices around us cheer.

Adam, laughing, hands me another Budweiser and toasts to the launch. I ask him about his earplugs—nobody else seems to be wearing them. Plus it feels unnatural for Adam, who subsists on two packs of smokes a day and a handle of whiskey, to be taking such physical precautions.

"I have tinnitus," he says.

"What?"

"Tinnitus. It's the medical term for chronic ear ringing. I played in hardcore bands all throughout high school and college."

"What do you mean by ear ringing?" I have never heard of such a thing.

"It's like a constant high-pitched frequency buzzing in my ears—mostly my left. I've had it for years."

"And you hear this *all* the time?" I am shocked.

Adam nods.

A few vehicles arrive, and a handful of others head towards us, carrying coolers, lawn chairs, and their own launching equipment. A hawk glides effortlessly through the lurid blue sky. The brightness, even beneath my sunglasses, feels excruciating. I ask Adam for his flask. Charlie asks if I have anything to launch, and I feel like I'm blanking—I search my pockets, feel my wrists and neck for jewelry—nothing—and the scrounge through my

The Fifth Wall

dusty backpack. I pull out *The Birth of Tragedy*, knowing I'll never read it, and hand it to Charlie. Adam assures me he has a copy somewhere on his shelf at home. A constant high-pitched ringing in his ears for every second of every day of his life? Charlie examines the cover and shrugs.

As Charlie instructs me how to mount the rifled book into the launching device, I think about the Oracle, and Mal's almost secretive affection for it—this intimate venue of communicating with forces unknown. And here, this launching up into space—this almost *dire* method of physical interaction—literally bypassing the Earth's atmosphere into the vastness of the unknown. Then there's Caleb, who ingests a combination of plants that thrust him up into similar spaces, where he claims to be able to converse with DNA, perceive auras, and communicate with spirits and the dead. I try to imagine myself hearing a sharp piercing consistently for the rest of my life, but I can't—it's too painful. Adam had explained that it's processed in his brain like an external noise, but really it is coming from within—a lack of hearing processed in the brain as sound. A ghost in his machinery.

I prop up the launching device with both hands, angling my face away from the piercing sun as Charlie counts down from five. Adam's fingers brush my lower back. Four. All these times when I think the only sound between us is the intensity communicated between our eyes and bodies—three—it is there, the sound. Two. Invisibly present and silent to everyone but him. One.

We lay on top of hot black metal, arms and legs spread wide, our drunken bodies desert angels in a sweltering invisible snow. We watch the sun set from a striking overlook onto sand dunes and cacti, a cascade of pink-yellow-blue enveloping the mountains, casting their shadows over the dark valley below.

After launching *The Birth of Tragedy*, we waited over two

hours, but never saw it fall. Often the objects end up as far as four to five miles away, in some stranger's backyard, or in the middle of the flat, open earth. I imagine the pages falling over bleeding red poppies, scattering amongst their blooming brightness, or caught in an orbit around the dying, spinning Earth. I take in the landscape and the beauty of the dimming sky, trying to picture the machines orbiting around this great planet, like mirrors of the Earth's existence—rather, Earth's billion-dollar "selfie" apparatuses, now equipped with cameras that can reveal invisible systems from galactic altitudes, all the way down to the incremental. We confirm our existence over and over, constantly place ourselves in a specific place and time—the planet as our stage, and the audience everywhere. With machines that mimic the body and mind with sensors that now *have sense*, we don't really have to be alive anymore to see. Is this the endpoint to our exploration—how we're going to die out? The Second Coming, in actuality, will be scientists turning nature inside out, cloning it, and running their program alongside of it? A dead world made to look alive.

Adam turns to me and tells me that he got my email. I ask him what he's talking about—I haven't written him any email. He says the one that I sent to him very late one evening from New York, nearly three years ago. He received it, and read it—in fact, many times over. I turn away with humiliation, going back to that awful moment in a time of desperation, now rewriting the past from that point up until now, before thinking that he'd passed over it, disregarded it, thought absolutely nothing of it...

"It actually really turned me on," he says.

I stare at him. Then I ask him why he didn't respond.

"I honestly wasn't emotionally invested."

"Ouch."

"You were *so* young, and you didn't realize it. I knew I couldn't in good conscience pursue you with any seriousness. Plus I was in the middle of a PhD—I didn't have much of myself to give."

The Fifth Wall

I return to the evening of the party. This was the August after my freshman year, just a couple of months after my class that Adam taught had ended. I'd made friends with a bunch of Berkeley grad students in the art department, and showed up one evening to an end-of-summer party in Oakland. We'd sort of kept in touch through a few emails about films and books—I made sure to try to intellectually impress, as I'd never met a man who stimulated me that way—by means of such intellect that motivated my artistic practice—and who was also quite charming, and of course retained a position of academic power. His interest in me was obvious, but I'd had little practice in reading men. I had an older boyfriend in high school who would light candles every time we fucked, which I at first found thoughtful, but then realized, with growing disgust, that it was an image of romance fed to him by romantic comedies he consumed like candy during childhood. The candles would often burn down onto his wooden dresser, and all I'd be thinking about while this half-hardened phallus pushed inside of me was that the room would catch on fire and that his mom would walk in and find us copulating and scream and order us to run for our lives, forcing us to escape buck naked onto the Berkeley city streets! I'd showed up to the party with a male friend I naively and consistently used as a potential third wheel, and had run into Adam, near-wasted, sitting on a porch railing, smoke encircling him, a drink in stock position in his other hand. The whole night was ours. We talked about everything from our childhoods and interests to the analysis of Ingmar Bergman's *The Seventh Seal*. I'd fantasized sexually about teachers before, having always connected with passionate older men. But this was different—I'd been pining for months, creating scenarios and instances of our eventual running-ins over and over until Adam became almost intangible—a sheer shadow in a memory of a future that never existed. We stayed at the party until very, very late—long after BART had stopped running, and Adam offered to drive me back to the Berkeley campus. I'd always refused to get in a car with anyone who had been drinking, but Adam was a fabulous drunk driver. He smoked and drove and blasted obscure hardcore music, going on and on about the history of the band and the scene and the style. My heart was out of my chest by then—I watched it pumping on the dashboard, while an opportune wetness leaked out of me, quite possibly all over the seat. I was living in the dorms then, and we sat in his truck outside for a while, talking nonsense, until I awkwardly asked him in. He was so drunk by then. He was stumbling and muttering and looked almost anachronistic in the very quiet student building—because it was summer, and most kids went home or away, but I'd stayed there because I couldn't stand to live alone with my mother and her horrible habits—the constant TV, the nagging, and then the random bursts of energy that always freaked me out—Adam had followed me up to my dorm, examining the horrible campus art, stumbling along the carpeted hallways until we finally made it to my bedroom, where he became aggressive and I tried to play along. We were both drunk, but he was much further gone. After trying for a while to get it up, he finally gave up and pushed me off of him, and we stared silently at each other for a long time. I was so *happy* to have him in my bed that I didn't even care about the outcome—I didn't really understand what was going on. He kept looking at me with this expression of inexplicable inquiry, as if waiting for me to say or do something that I wasn't saying or doing. But my fantasies had morphed the whole appalling scenario into an event that couldn't be anything *but* romantic. This, here, was true romance. This was what I'd been waiting for. He'd then passed out and later left while I was sleeping—I'd woken up only to the traces of fuzzy memories of his being there, wondering if it even happened at all.

Why do you deny yourself a sense of wonder? This line suddenly comes back to me, flooding through my brain—a comment that Adam had made to me earlier that evening at the party. What had I possibly been talking about to receive such a peculiar question?

I look over at Adam's splayed body, collecting the desert's energy like a sponge. Studying his face, I make out visible pock marks and pores, a shaving scar beneath his earlobe, his skin projecting a gray sheen undoubtedly from all the constant American Spirits and Jameson handles that feed his withering body—the image of his saggy ball sack bouncing against my ass during sex. Is this romance—rather, his *sense of wonder?* Would we even be sitting here under this brilliant, blazing sky without the chemicals—the toxicity raging through our lonely bodies in these ever-so-heartrending attempts at some sort of closeness? Adam Black and his theories on human existence and cinematic history—a failed artist himself, with dozens of unfinished films lining the very end of his wall-lined bookshelves, which I'd recently asked him about, but he grazed over the story with a few anecdotes about his academic brain outweighing his own artistry, and then quickly changed the subject. Have I always put so much weight onto men? The power that they instill in me feels so near to what I imagine a religious experience. A sort of idolatry of one male human into a force that moves through my every day—this magical, God-like presence stimulating my actions and thoughts, fueling my existence. Even years later, through semi-serious relationships—mostly badly-ending—in college and then grad school, Adam had never fully left my mind—perhaps because I'd never allowed myself to remember what actually happened properly.

Perhaps the Lacks—like the tinnitus—aren't spaces of absence or forgetting, but are more like reminders of my physical existence ... my body communicating with me, screaming at me that I'm *here*.

My mother, for years distracting herself with back-to-back television shows—*Oprah, Maury, Seinfeld, Frasier*—anything to numb her increasing neuroses. A welcomed form of submission, the mind's way of controlling the body. I feel a buzz in my back pocket and check my phone, but there are still no service bars—a phantom vibration.

A tumor can appear in an instant, like a magic trick—a silver coin from an ear canal, a white rabbit from a black top hat. All of a sudden it's there, like the dust from the ground and God's quick breath into Adam's nostrils in the creation myths of man. Fully manifested and destined to fall. Was it her body's way of sending a message? A last straw, a final warning? Had it been sending her messages all along, but that she just couldn't translate?

We use technology in place of our own coping mechanisms, denying ourselves the reality of the present moment. And now we've become too comfortable within these images—these deceptive comforts of a life unlived—to the point where we're losing our most important sense. But it's not sight that's disappearing; it's our sensation—our ability to feel.

You think you control your body until it turns against you. Perhaps the shooting was her last attempt at gaining the upper hand, of destroying the intruder. An explosion to cover up the implosion—the bomb that already existed inside. The origins of the Lack.

Deirdre Ackerman
Tumor, 2013
Cancerous cells, brain, blood, you know, etcetera...

That night in a hotel room in Barstow, I am bent over the bed, forehead near the floor, my rear up and thrust out towards a fierce, thwacking body. Adam clenches my hips with his pointy fingertips, his scraping, chewed-off nails. The carpet chafes my elbows. He's pounding away with a force from somewhere else entirely, somewhere inside of himself, out and away from the scene. A drive that seems wholly unconcerned with me.

It's something that, when it's happening, you just know. The energies hurl towards each other, but miss by a hair, both headed for a direction well beyond the other.

He is saying to me, "You like my hard cock in your pussy?" He is yanking back my hair. "You like this, huh? Don't you?" He is saying this from somewhere else.

I am thinking, *yes, isn't it obvious? Although my head's this close to smacking the floor, I have a lot of really great nerve endings right now.*

I allow my motions to translate.

Adam arches over me so that I can feel his torso against my back. He pulls me back up onto the bed and our bodies readjust, straighten out, continue.

"Tell me why you like to have sex with me." His voice is soft and demanding, urgent in tone.

"What?" I muffle into the comforter, thinking I've misheard.

"Tell me why you like having sex with me." He pulls out and twists me around so we're face to face.

Perhaps I attract these violent men because I subconsciously desire the emotionally unavailable. The drama, the consequences. The act without the act.

"Uhhh..." I try to force myself to speak but instead I choke on air. *Because my body is attracted to your body, and you have a fairly large dick?* I cough and turn to the side, pounding on my chest.

"You okay over there?"

It feels like I am swallowing sand. Like if I closed my eyes and reopened them we'd be submerged in sand, the bed would be a dune. The sky would open up to a limitless expanse of space and air, and time would fall and shatter into granules, coagulate the room with a desert heaviness.

"Sheila?"

"I'm fine!"

Adam lets go and allows my movements to dictate his. I breathe in and wiggle my hair out of my face, twist and sit up, straddle his body, lean my face in.

How it is possible to be gazing at a person and have multiple limbs touching, external organs buzzing, and not see him at all.

"Is this okay?" I ask him.

"Sure."

"Okay."

"Do you feel anything?"

"Sure."

"I mean if you're not feeling much, we can change it up."

"No no, it's fine," he says.

I am not sure what my expression is but by the slight raising of his brows and his slanted look, I sense a closing-off, a retreating.

My unresponsiveness. My inability to express, my unwillingness to play. It all begins to culminate into a debilitating anxiety. Maybe I'm not intoxicated enough. My body is just so exhausted.

I'm now propping myself over him, balancing on my wrists and knees. It is at moments like these when the sex becomes literal; organs become organs inside and outside other organs. The action dies down to a stillness. You start to really listen.

It's either listen or disrupt the juncture. Be the one to move.

Because it won't be long until the landscape beyond the bed returns, before the desert fades into sharp angles and stark fluorescent lighting.

"Sex talk is just not my forte," I try to explain. "It's one of those things that I don't *not* like hearing—I mean, I think it can be really sexy sometimes, I really do. But I kind of freeze up. It's like how I can't read comic books—the text and the illustrations—they're just way too much simultaneously. I get so overwhelmed that the page becomes one big blurry jumble of information and I end up not being able to see anything at all."

He taps me on the hip and I pull myself off him, bounce over to his left. We face each other sideways. He's looking at me as if I am all the way across the room. He's trying to figure me out.

I reach over and touch his forearm. Nothing on his body responds.

"I'm sorry." I sigh.

"Don't worry about it," he says. "We just lost the jive, it happens." He smiles awkwardly and closes his eyes, wraps his arm around my torso and pulls me in. I think of ten thousand things I could say at this moment, and another thousand I could *do* without saying. But instead I remain silent, still, wondering where the flask went.

Adam moves over me like an alligator. His head rests on my stomach, his body extended and still. I am playing with his hair and he is playing "I'm-in-a-partial-coma." He sprouts from my torso, a massive, heavy limb.

We sink into the bed. About five minutes of silence pass.

The failure of this art comes when the connection tricks me— as it never fails to do—when my body mistakes these practiced, unfeigned motions as *love*. When the feeling overwhelms the situation, when what art is supposed to induce in us and yet always, and forever, fails to—the boundaries collapse, the object disappears.

And what's left is the desire for the part of myself that I've just lost, now mistaken as him—the setting lingering before me like a mirage—the Lack that's actually been inside me since the beginning.

Upon returning home the following afternoon, I open my Mac-Book. I click on the camera icon and the live surveillance feed comes into view. A barren dirt flatbed fills the screen. Gone are the hedges and plants and grasses aligning our front and back lawns; only the larger trees remain, framing the plot like lonely skyscrapers.

I slam my fist on the desk. Why don't I feel anything? Perhaps my brain can't process the house's literal absence from this kind of distance?

On my phone are two voicemails—one from Jesse, and the other, my dad. The deconstruction is completed—hooray!—and Jesse was able to salvage about sixty-five percent of the materials, which was much more than he expected, considering the overall damage. And my dad has invited me to dinner on his boat tomorrow night. By the blatant concern in his voice, it's obvious Robby called him.

I walk down the hall to Mal's room, where I find her in the midst of unpacking from her retreat. I collapse onto her bed with gestured exaggeration.

"How was the double truth weekend?" I ask.

"Oh, very relaxing, very open...well, kind of odd, actually."

"Why was it odd?"

"I don't know—I think maybe I'm just done with retreats."

"What do you mean? What about your whole monologue about how useful they are? You almost had me convinced."

"They're definitely useful, up to a certain point. Then you kind of realize that the rest of the work to be done is actually outside of the naked near-orgies—which are certainly marvelous

The Fifth Wall

in their own right, don't get me wrong—but after a while they don't really... I don't know... satisfy?"

"Speaking of orgies," I say, "what's the craziest thing that someone's ever said to you during sex?"

Mal pauses to consider this while folding a pair of bright turquoise leggings. *"I want to murder you,"* she says.

"You've got to be kidding me."

"I was like—*how are you so absurdly good at this?*"

We both crack up.

She asks me why the specific question and I spill the whole story about Adam, the Drog, and the desert, and then about Jesse and The Lacks and then the deconstruction's whole anticlimactic finale. By the end of my diatribe she has her head in her hands, yanking down her face-skin in a gesture of dire distress.

"My *God*, Sheila—that's a *lot* for just two and a half *weeks!*"

I moan into her furry bedspread.

Her phone vibrates discordantly on a wooden desk. "Apparently the Oracle has something to say about this." She clears her throat. *"The angel of death functions, cold and conditionally, in canine worlds in the outskirts of the city."*

"You know, it sounds sort of like blackout poetry," I mumble.

"What's that?"

I turn my head to the side. "It's where you literally black out lines in a book to create poems out of already-existing words on a page—it's a technique of appropriation that started in the sixties with the beat poets in North Beach."

Mal scrolls through the Oracle's previous text messages with a stern look on her face. "No," she shakes her head, "I will not accept that simple of an origin."

I laugh.

"The Oracle can't just be simplified to a random composition of words!"

"I wonder what would happen if you sent it a selfie."

"Hmm, like a sexy selfie?"

"Any kind of selfie," I say.

"I think that would kind of defeat the whole point."

A quiet knock resounds from behind Mal's half-open door.

"Yes?" says Mal, loudly.

Dustin pokes his head in. "Have you guys seen the video?" His oily face glows with evident fascination.

We simultaneously shake our heads no.

He slithers in, guardedly, his feet invisible beneath his gaping jeans, and holds out his iPad for us to see. We hover around the screen. The caption says GOOGLE GLASS CAPTURES VIDEO OF MAN BEATING WOMAN IN SAN FRANCISCO BAR; it has over three million views. Dustin presses play. It is an eight-and-a-half minute video filmed from a woman's Google Glass as she enters a bar in the Lower Haight District. A young, hipster-looking dude approaches the camera (the woman) holding a glass filled with what looks like vodka and soda, which splashes around as he gestures to us. He is obviously drunk. At first he starts poking fun at us—asking why we're wearing such a stupid looking gadget. The woman's voice at first responds jokingly as well, saying she works at a start up that gave her a free model to try out. When the teasing continues and becomes increasingly hostile, she asks him to politely leave her alone. The hipster—who is very, very drunk now—gets very, very angry, and begins to try to swipe them off our face. We swat at him, shouting *hey—come on now!* And he quickly becomes more violent. *Do you think it's fun to record us now?* He starts to shout at us as he slaps us in the face, and the camera becomes shaky from us ducking and turning from side to side. A knee shoots up and into our stomach as we keel over, coughing. A crowd forms around us and tackles the man to the ground. Bodies shout obscenities—a few women try to go at the man, while others actually start screaming at the camera, shrieking that Google Glass is an invasion to their right to privacy. Then there's a lot of static and commotion and the video shuts off.

The Fifth Wall

For a while none of us say anything.

"I feel like there's something large and terrible happening," says Mal, softly. "I've felt it in this city for months. Something deep and dire that none of us can possibly control."

"Are you talking about gentrification?" Dustin sniffs.

"I feel it, too," I say. "The feeling that at any day, at any moment, something really horrible could happen."

Mal reaches out and strokes my arm.

"Cities go through ebbs and flows," says Dustin. "It's just in the process of learning how to act now with all of this money at its disposal."

Mal glares at him.

"What's interesting about this woman," he says, "is that she's begun this sort of war that we haven't really seen before. One of, like, civil rights and privatized technology. What are we allowed to document? Just as we walk down the street and observe life, do we not have the right to record it, and save it, and display it publicly to all? As technology becomes smaller and smaller, the boundaries between the public and private are beginning to disappear. It's fascinating, really."

Mal clears her throat. "So you think this *violence* is a good thing? This poor woman—albeit a stupid fucking idiot for thinking she could walk into *McCormick's* wearing *Google Glass*—deserves to be beaten up for the sake of modern day society? Isn't that always the argument for violence against women—we become this sort of *archetype* that's useful in storytelling later on?"

"That's not what I'm saying at all. I don't see it as good *or* bad." Dustin looks at me for help, and I signal him a brief look of commiseration. "It's just very telling, is all. The whole fact that this was all caught on camera."

"And from a first person point of view," I add, quietly.

Mal gives me *the look*.

I shrug.

"Exactly." Dustin nods. "It totally changes how the media presents information. This is a really exciting time to be alive."

I watch Mal bite her tongue, her face reddening. I think about how interesting of an addition to *The Last Art* this video would be, if mounted in the "Distraction" room, as part of one of the thousands of other moments caught in real time. Just a week ago I was helping install the work of a video artist who worked for Microsoft's Bing Maps Platform, which allows organizations and developers worldwide to create applications for their businesses layered on top of licensed map imagery. His job was to compile data from images taken by aerial cameras and satellite sensors to build 3D city models and terrain. A "virtual topologist," they called him. A "geospatial engineer." He was present throughout the installation, adamant in overseeing the process. He stood behind me as I measured out spaces on the wall for the flat screen monitors that would project his designs.

We are recording the whole world, he had said to me.

And I said, *You are literally putting people 'on the map.'*

This is what art's become, he said. *A virtual simulacrum, an information rig.*

I had wanted to reply that the notion of art was changing— that to be a contemporary artist was not necessarily to identify yourself with the medium, as a painter, or sculptor creating something unseen—as a recluse from society—but now as a revealer of what was already there, in new combinations of forms and images, a person both inside and outside of space and time. He was writing the history of the world in his art, which, to him, *was not art.*

But I was busy trying to mount a thirty-pound flat screen to the wall, while he just stood beside me and watched.

People are still surprised by the 3D aspect, how much it looks the same. How much it looks real, he just kept on going. *I was once a filmmaker, you know.*

The Fifth Wall

Oh yeah? I grunted.

And now a replicator of worlds, he said.

"Anyway." Dustin gathers his iPad and makes for the door. "It's back to work for me." He slinks awkwardly out of the room. I look over at Mal solemnly. She approaches me with a welcomed embrace. I fall into her body like a lump of melting clay. The ride back with Adam had been severely uncomfortable—something between our energies was severed; the air in the truck felt sparse and stale, congested with pockets of awkward silence, shortening the length of my breaths, like we were competing for oxygen. He dropped me off at my house with an engine idling and a quick "talk to you soon."

"Poor Sheila." Mal sighs and rubs my back with solid, heavy strokes. "You got what you wanted, didn't you dear? How horrible."

Strawberry Way winds up a raised plateau in the illustrious Berkeley Hills; trees and shrubs and wild messes of dark yellows and greens connect large properties, hug the houses with natural softness, project an image of suburban well-being.

I approach my own Ground Zero cautiously, while heaving from the steep incline.

Here, Sheila, is your very own hole. A glorified, materialized *Monster Lack.*

I plop down in front of the plot of hollow land, contemplating the absence of the house, and still not believing it—still somehow processing the change as temporary.

It's as if a glitch is happening in the landscape before me, a flicker of an image. A white rabbit in a magician's hat.

Now you see it, now you don't.

It's similar to how I felt when the beheading videos surfaced online in 2004. I heard about them and I thought, this is the most terrifying thing I can think of to witness (though it isn't anymore). This is inhuman, I thought, despicable, power-driven madness. I will not watch that. Never *ever*, cross my heart, fucking *bastards*.

But then I thought, I can't believe that this exists. I can't believe that people are watching these accounts of violence, these archival shorts of terror. Why do they keep watching them? What do they think they'll see?

What people are looking for on the Internet these days are signs of familiarity. Evidence that they exist. Bing Maps is the extreme state of this. A new temporality. An accelerated stasis of the present.

A cloud blocks the sun, and for a second I'm covered in its shadow. Chirping swallows. Rustling ferns. A lawn mower stirs in the background. A car's engine. A man shouting to his wife.

Why is it that I cannot experience this setting as *real?* What is different now that wasn't before? What is so off about this scene?

The truth is when you have the option to see something that you think you know you'd never want to see, you will watch it anyway. The mystery is too much to handle.

People go crazy searching their own homes on the Internet, the Bing Maps guy went on. *They get hard-ons the second the image of their lawn pops up on the screen. Like they've never seen it before. Like somehow their lawn was shrunken to a miniature size and they're now God looking down from heaven. Like it's magic, or something.*

What happens is you click the link that's right there in front of you, underlined and bolded, and blinking swollen red. You click the link and before you opens a page with a rectangular black box formatted like a viewfinder, with a circular symbol in the center, a text that reads *loading…* You click ▶ and the image flickers to a surprisingly well-lit room. It is a room like any other room. The camera focuses straight-shot on the victim affixed to the chair in center stage. The victim recites his name and the names of his family members, his voice effortless and

The Fifth Wall

monotone. It's like he's staring straight at you but not actually seeing you, or acknowledging that you're there. The image is cropped so that at the bottom of the screen is the victim's torso, the sides about a half a finger's length of empty, gray space. The night before her suicide, I picture my mother brushing her teeth. She stands in front of the mirror, straight-faced and still, except for the movement of her wrist sliding the tooth-brush back and forth across her teeth. Her skin is pale under the three bright bulbs that align the mirror's top edge. Her pupils are dilated. Her eyebrows trimmed. Her hair up and parted slightly to the left.

I don't know why I see this particular image. It is just what comes to mind.

Scene change to the same room but now the victim is sitting on the floor, his hands and feet secured. Five masked men stand behind him, only their eyes visible. The one in the center recites something from two stapled pieces of paper. There is a time marker on the bottom right hand screen.

You know what's going to happen before it even begins.

You walk in the door and there she is.

The staging's constructed. The set-up is calculated. The reciting continues, and you note from the video that it is five-and-a-half minutes long, but since you are only on minute one-and-fifteen-seconds, you have a while to go. But still your eyes are peeled.

She just pauses, drops, and smacks on the floor.

You think, I am watching this and I am starting to cry but I don't understand this feeling in my body, because it's not that I've never seen anything like this, it's not surprise or aston-ishment or anger or fear or even guilt. It's more like a type of dread, the knowledge inside you that you've seen this before, millions of times, in movies, on TVs, on the Internet, on screens. It's the feeling that you are literally having to tell yourself the entire time that this is really happening—rather, this has really happened, in *real life*, that someone has actually died this way, experienced the kind of fear you realize you've only seen and experienced from afar, and that it's a whole different type of fear that you can't comprehend, because it's the format that seems to be tricking you, the characters, and staging, the removal of setting, and space, and time.

While you wait for the ambulance, you pace around. From one room to another and back around again. The house has been reduced to a state of ruin. Every object is broken down, every part now labeled in your mind. This is a *table*, Sheila, this is a *leg*. The house loses all function without her. This material is *wood*, a combination of *oak* and *chestnut*. This is a *square*. This is a *screw*. Like the space of a bedroom, an office, a studio—the more space you have, the more chaotic it becomes. Four bedrooms, two-and-a-half bathrooms, a living room, dining room, kitchen, breakfast nook, foyer, garage, garden, portable greenhouse... every object is coded, now, with the presence of the dead.

The masked men begin singing and chanting. The tension increases. Suddenly there's quick movement. The victim is sideways and the men surround him. One man holds the boy's body from behind; the other saws his neck. The camera zooms in so that his head fills the screen.

Someone is zooming in with the button on a camera. Someone is aware of how to capture a close-up—the tension that a close-up creates.

This, says my mother's doctor, pointing to an X-ray, *is the Glioblastoma Multiforme—what we like to call the "white elephant" of tumors. It's situated between the frontal and temporal lobes.* The doctor uses his fingers to encircle my mother's brain. *They are unfortunately often asymptomatic before reaching maximum size, as was the case with Deirdre.* He looks at me gravely. *I sat down with her and discussed all the treatment options—maximal surgical resection of the tumor, chemotherapy, and also even experimental Gamma Knife radiosurgeries and boron neutron*

The Fifth Wall

therapies... there was a whole list we talked about. We sat down and systematically created a road map of plans...

You are equally surprised and not surprised at how long it takes to saw off his head. You wonder at what point does the victim actually stop feeling the pain, and at what point he actually dies. Because his mouth is open and his eyes are peeled, fixated on nothing and nowhere, arrested in a state of fear.

This is the corner where I, Sheila, age ten, tripped on Tracy (our old Maine Coon), and twisted my right ankle. It swelled to the size of a baseball. For a week I gave my parents hell.

This is where Caleb practiced the cello.

Here is where my mother cried when my dad's father died.

This is my mother's favorite chair.

This is a chair.

As you walk through the house, you notice how different the rooms look once familiarity begins to dwindle, the objects becoming solely functional, their existence black and white.

Is this really a synthetic fabric? My mother didn't care for synthetic fabrics.

When the masked man finally cuts his way through, after almost twenty seconds of torment, of visible process, honest and brutal action captured in real time, and raises it up by the hair, beaming faceless with defeat, when the mantras become deafening, and the body behind the camera begins shaking so that the image destabilizes, its focus unsteady, the culminating energy spasmodic, all-consuming, when the video just stops and leaves you stranded in the moment, all you're left with is a feeling, an odd sense of detachment. You are here but you're somehow changed, you've *been through* something, experienced a horror that is no longer part of you (and never even was to begin with), and that it's *left* you, abandoned you like a lover.

Oh, Sheila, why can't you just *mourn* already? Here you are, now—sitting in front of the foundation of the dwelling you spent eighteen years and change in, wishing you were feeling more of a sense of loss. But you know very well that the house was barely recognizable to begin with—it disappeared right with the bullet. She created her own tomb.

Up in the Marin Headlands, riding is a different experience. The air is denser, thick with molecules you can feel as you push through them. The scents of tea tree and eucalyptus, fresh salt and dirt.

After you cross the Golden Gate Bridge and move beyond the places most tourists can't reach without rented vehicles, or walking—it becomes an elevated expanse of natural, embodied slithering. Saturated greens amidst the bay's sapphire vastness. Up and down and once you're set in motion it's like the pedals are what's moving you forward, the quadratic burn only a reminder from your body that you are here, enveloped in air.

The best route is to bike around the entrance towards the tunnel that leads to the valley of the headlands. The tunnel is one consistent incline, but once you're through, it's like you're in Kansas, or the projection of. Simple houses separated by fences and thicket, with dense, clinging dew. And then up the winding hills you go.

The wind is stronger the higher and higher you get. But just keep pedaling—pedal as fast as you can, the wind through your ears like bellowing, deep breaths, until it feels like too much oxygen. Gasping and gasping and pedaling and pedaling until the ground releases you from its stronghold, disappears so that you fall.

The late afternoon sun pierces the bay's skyline, forming retinal dots along the tops of soft, rippling waves. Below deck, my father and I sit across from one another on plush leather seating in the booth of the boat's compact kitchenette, eating fresh seared codfish and sautéed vegetables over hearty brown rice. Pozzo curls up in his doggie bed beside me, his stump an odd composition of bulbous tissue, hair and skin.

"Tumors aren't genetic, Sheila—this is not something that you should be worrying about." My father meticulously examines a bite of codfish, making sure all the tiny bones are picked out. I sip his homemade pinot noir and stare at the tall stacks of books lining the walls behind him. I knew I shouldn't have even tried.

"Your mother took all her vitamins, she practiced yoga, she meditated—she hardly ever touched red meat. She smoked a little pot in college, sure, but so did everyone. We both enjoyed cocaine for about three minutes before it got old. She caught a lot of colds working at the hospital, but that's to be expected, which probably made her even stronger. What I mean to say is that she did everything right. Your mother was neurotic, but for the most part she really took care of herself." He chews the cod and swallows. "What's more likely is you'll get arthritis starting in your early thirties—," he points his fork at me, "I have it, my mother had it, my mother's father had it—my uncle has it. There's some heart disease in the family, but once you get old, the heart gets old, and malfunctions are perfectly natural. Cancer is different—there are so many factors that can contribute to it that have absolutely nothing to do with genetics. If I remember correctly the house she grew up in was right near a nuclear waste site..." He looks up but then shakes his head at the notion. "Anyway, my point being: you can't *catch* a tumor."

I watch my father pour himself some more wine and shift uncomfortably in his seat. I notice his body's grown slimmer, more muscular—he appears larger, his size perhaps compromised by the dimensions of the boat. He's grown a bushy beard, multicolored, scraggly. He wears cargo pants and a mesh parka.

I ask him if he read Caleb's most recent lengthy text.

The Fifth Wall

"Of course I read it. The kid's having some experiences out in places that have the tendency to seep into your head. I took LSD in the sixties—I'm not a foreigner to blasting off. But there comes a point where you have to distinguish between what's real and what's useful. I knew I was raising sensitive children from the day each of you was born. And the real fact of the matter is that the kid needed to find an alternative to heroin—at least this new nonsense is more sustainable."

"The kid you're speaking about is thirty-five, Dad."

"Which is exactly my point."

I breathe in deeply, feel tension forming in my throat. My eyes search the room for another focal point—piles of neatly coiled ropes, a fire extinguisher, life vests, inflatable rafts, cases of spring water. It's as if my father's preparing for the apocalypse. His life has become a practice of efficiency, a series of tasks and tests asserting some form of concreteness, some reassurance of humanity. It is at times like this, as the light wanes through the ship's portholes, and the air becomes cooler, that nature takes over our senses, blinds us from sensibility, our relation to the outside turning foreign and gray. Anxiety sets in, slithers around my organs.

"Now tell me about what happened at the museum," he says.

I place my utensils down, pausing to think carefully about my response. "I'm not exactly sure." It's at times like these when I want to turn to him and scream.

"Oh you're not fooling me. I could recognize that expression from a mile away, even in my old age."

It's been inside of me forever, I wish I could explain. *I feel it every day—death, like a vital organ. My body constantly on the verge of some sort of terror. How her death only brought it to the surface. The feeling of my brain exploding with a bullet—how the life inside me could blacken out in an instant.*

How does one exist, with this constant awareness? How does one choose to live?

"I don't . . . I don't seem to have the right language to explain it," I say.

My dad sighs and lifts up a forkful of food. "You know, language was born in Tragedy—it started with the monologue. The actor spoke directly to the audience, even when addressing another actor, from which of course dialogue developed and corrupted everything. But in a monologue, there's no co-ownership of words, no displacement of direction or meaning—the actor's perspective is the whole world."

"Like a suicide note?" I say, looking up. "Which she didn't even have the decency to leave?"

My father pauses. "Your mother was obviously not thinking clearly."

Like the victim being forced to recite his name and the names of his family members into the camera—his last speech to the world. Or the video of my mother's head talking to the camera, the words drowning out in the incredible static, her face now merely a surface masking actions, her motions fixed and endlessly repeatable. The terror in technology.

"I've been watching this home video I found of you filming Mom—it was dated a few years after Caleb was born. You work this extreme close-up on her face and then ask her a question—which the tape only catches in a low, indiscernible mumble—and then Mom looks into the camera and mouths something that I can't make out because the tape's too warped." I look him in the eyes. "And I feel like it's something *really important*. I don't know how else to explain it. I just have to know what she's saying. Like the whole world depends on it."

My dad sighs. "I understand that you're searching for clues and signs in all the places you can find—but you have to get it in your head, Sheila, that some things are just left unanswered. There was a tumor, yes. Did we know about it? No. Is that your fault? No. Is that my fault? Certainly not. Is it her fault? Well, there could be some pretty good arguments in favor of that one.

The Fifth Wall

But that's not the point. The point is that it was out of your
control. And you have to live in the aftermath of it, whether
you like it or not."
    I slam my fists down on the table. The whole cabin shakes.
"There's no way that you couldn't have known! I know her, and
I *know* she would have told you!"
    My father's eyes become wide, bulging.

                    DANIEL
                 (eyes wide, bulging)
        As much as you would like to pin this on
        me—which is totally unreasonable and also
        very *beneath* you—the fact of the matter
        is that whether you choose to believe it
        or not, your mother was a fatalist—and she
        always had been, since the day I met her.
        She *gave up*, Sheila. She couldn't handle
        it, and she didn't want to face it, so
        there wasn't really another option for her,
        was there? And even if she had told me,
        do you think I could talk that woman out
        of anything? This was a woman who feared
        death so much that she became a nurse just
        to try to have *some* control over it. She
        couldn't handle med school, so she chose
        an easier route. And here's something you
        probably don't know—when I met her, she
        was actually enrolled in *art school*. Yes,
        art school. Isn't that surprising? And she
        couldn't handle that, either—she could
        never give herself fully to anything...
        so in this regard, I'm actually kind of
        impressed by her willingness to go through
        with such an abominable act. Actions

without practical use terrified her—anything
where she had to be alone for a period
of time in her own brain. And oh, what a
beautiful brain she had, when she could
let go and *enjoy* herself. I knew I married
a difficult person in the beginning, but
really I had no idea. I thought I'd be the
one to relieve her of all those fears—but
that's how we think when we're young. All
we see are mirrors. The being we project
onto the other person is never real. Back
then I used to take a lot of close-ups.
I used to really love the camera—which is
of course where you get it from. I always
carried that thing around with me—what
a magnificent invention! A living time
capsule, right there in front of our eyes.
And your mother was so beautiful. I just
loved her little thin face. And she looked
so good on camera—you know, certain people,
they just eat up the screen. You're not old
enough to really remember what it was like
before cameras, but let me tell you—once
we had them, there was no turning back.
They hold a mythic quality that the theater
never had. Do I think cameras killed the
theater? Yes, of course they did. It was
bound to happen. But the theater will
always be an art of the living, and film
an art of the dead. The images look alive,
but they're only fooling you. The problem
with you kids today is you make everything
more complex than it needs to be. I see it
all the time with my students—these young

The Fifth Wall

artists who think they're the first ones
to have radical ideas about technology,
society—let me tell you something. I was
talking to Robby on the phone, and he was
telling me about that new Richard Serra
sculpture. This is a fucking perfect
example. And stop your crying, Sheila—you
need to get it together. Simple gestures,
simple lines. That's what the whole
multimillion-dollar piece of steel comes
down to. I'll tell you what. A "torqued
ellipse" is just a horizontal line that's
slightly bent. The simpler the design, the
more complex it is. The more room there
is to *imagine*. I remember you calling me
from school. You said Dad, *Dad*—at Cornell
all our seminar discussions are about
failure—all anyone's ever talking about
is how the medium of art is inherently a
failure to represent reality, that we're
all now creating art with this knowledge
of failure already present, already built
into our work—you *hated* it, Sheila, you
thought, when can we get to the *actual*
work? In grad school you just talk and talk
and talk. And I've built my life around
it, because I chose to be a historian,
because to me, talking about actors and
writing about actors is much easier than
actually *being* an actor—so in a sense, I'm
a real *failure*. Do you think I *don't* think
it wasn't a *nightmare* to walk into your
mother's house, hoping to surprise her,
and instead finding her brains spilling

Rachel Nagelberg

out? Do you think I wouldn't have given
up *everything* to have been able to trade
places with you—to *not* have you go through
that? I mean, *hell*—I'm not unfamiliar with
trauma—I've seen some things in my day—
we all see terrible things constantly on
the news. But this—I would never wish this
upon my worst enemy. Do you think that
I think you should be getting therapy? Yes,
very much so. I myself have stayed away
because it is my nature to do so—I am not
very talented at consoling. This is just
how I was raised. Your mother was the one
who was professionally trained to take
care of people. That was never my role.
Stop crying, for Christ's sake. What's
that? No—come on. You're not afraid of
death, Sheila—you're afraid of the movies.
You used to cry every time you watched
Peter Pan, for Christ's sake. Finish your
cod, Sheila—you're as skinny as a fucking
seahorse these days. It's time to start
taking better care of yourself. And it
starts here, with eating fresh, nutritious
food. And—hey, hey—laying a little off
of that wine over there. This isn't that
shitty stuff composed mostly of sugar. This
is the real deal. This is a recipe I've
been working on for years.

Artists act and make choices. They live and they make responses. They absorb the stimuli surrounding them. They don't justify anything.

People grow up with a unique set of references, learned belief systems, complex combinations of energies. We form images in our minds about what's right and what's wrong, and the possibilities in the gray area in-between.

Inconsistency within our own processes is important—it allows us to continue to live, to respond. The second we stop responding, we die.

In San Francisco, when the wind blows harshly, it forces one to ask why it feels like the Earth is punishing—is it the shifting tectonic forces, the dissolving of the ozone, the culminating grief in lost bodies thrashing through the streets?

There are coincidences, and then there are consequences. The difference depends on the preparation, the acknowledged foresight; the feeling that what is to come might very well be a whole lot worse. Or, perhaps it has already been this bad, but it's a horror that's become so familiar that you no longer see it.

When, then, does the trauma begin?

And where and when can it end?

For years I've been searching the male body as if there is something to find inside of it. Some tangible mass, some undiscovered organ, the magic rib from whence Eve became cloned. *This is now bone of my bones and flesh of my flesh . . .*

We go through motions, patterns; we make decisions about how to live.

To tell the truth, I've always felt as if I've been living in false positions, subsisting without contour. Perhaps that's why I'm drawn to obliteration. A false embodiment—all-consuming, but exceedingly short-lasting, never amounting to anything tangible.

But these days I feel a constant inner restlessness—as if I am a hollowed tree, surrounded by nocturnal animals that are foraging discarded objects and storing them inside of me. I feel born of a great absence. The air in my body feels strange. There's a constant feeling that something's missing, but what is too vague to really be sure...

To spend one's whole life searching for something elusive—something, anything, to cling to. Perhaps that's when the body makes the decision to create. The tumor, the Lacks, the tinnitus—all born from an absence. From a deep, assembling rage.

Caleb says he can feel depression deep inside his DNA—has seen visions of himself in the womb enveloped in dark, writhing energy, has felt the sadness of the cavernous body housing him, and how he fed on that sadness—*her* sadness—the only world he knew.

There are studies about mitochondria and the passing trauma from a mother to her child—how a body forms within a learned nervous system, the gut, the second brain of the human body that for some reason we've devolved in this country to neglect.

Isn't the body's main job to store things?

Performance artists believe that if you can push the body to its limit without dying, that death is no longer an inevitability, but an eventual consequence. I have never wished for such control. And yet, I've created my own ruin.

It was an appallingly horrific coincidence. I walked in the doorway, and there she was. I never wanted to step foot in that house again. Just knowing it was there made me so anxious I could hardly breathe.

If I'm a terrorist, then I should want something. I should want death and destruction, to induce fear in others, to brutally fight, to die for what I believe in.

But I don't really believe in anything, and I don't want to die. I used to think I wanted to—even as a little girl. I watched Peter Pan and I cried. I couldn't control the muscles in my face, my trembling body. To never grow old, to watch the world age around you. For a week I wet the fucking bed.

Pan, which is ironically the root of panic—to be consumed by it all.

I have this feeling deep inside me—this rush to get up and lunge at a great distance and purge myself of something that's not physically in my stomach or intestines, but somewhere lurking in my brain—the scariest part of it knowing that this feeling has been with me all along—this emptiness, this dread—this Lack spreading amongst my insides, throughout my veins and arteries, my organic flowing system, all around me and inside of me, like a desert swallowing me whole, and each day spitting out a copy of a copy of myself...

The fear that this is all that there is, and it's all that will ever be. Your life will never reach a certain point—the point keeps receding, like a moving landscape, disappearing into the distance—and you're always on the way.

All of history feels like it's culminating onto the moving image of her body, her face a pixilation of tiny moving pieces—black hole and white wall, screen and camera, always expanding, repeating, playing forever into madness.

We can't turn back, and we can never unsee.

This is something we have to live with.

The camera's still recording.

ACT THREE

"Do you think of yourself as doomed?"
ELI MOSCOWITZ, *The Fifth Wall*

"Now this was a time when there was no context—there was no hierarchy of history to look at. Making art was what you could do to engage your friends."

Richard Serra sits on stage facing the interviewer, Garrett Henderson, the Senior Curator of Painting and Sculpture at SFMoMA. Both are angled towards one another so that they partly face the audience, directing their conversation outwards, a structural gesture as if to say, "it's okay for you to listen in." A small rectangular coffee table rests between the two moss-colored velour high-backed armchairs, illuminated by overhead stage lights. Below them, an oriental rug of deep maroons and greens. Garrett crosses his legs academically, leans back and folds together swollen fingers, nods rhythmically. Richard Serra sips water from a mason jar.

"I was working for U.S. Steel building tresses. It fascinated me that no one was using steel the way it was used in the Industrial Revolution—for its weight, its durability. I've always taken my materials seriously."

Adam and I sit in the back of the Phyllis Wattis Theater, the prominent lecture hall on the first floor of SFMoMA. It's a small auditorium with two levels, the first a ground area seating about one hundred persons, the second a slanted, bleacher-like seating rising up about eleven rows, spanning the room's back wall. There is a thematic color scheme of taupes and sepias, creating an old-fashioned feel to the architecture—slightly monochromatic, fading with age.

Two days after the traumatic visit with my Dad, I'd received a voicemail from Robby offering me two tickets to the sold out Richard Serra lecture that coincided with *Band*'s opening. Apparently the Drog had been found the day after I left, collapsed in a heap of twitching parts, behind the finished partition that originally held it, making the whole horrible experience seem—Robby said—just like one big nightmare.

"It's about going back to the primitive way of thinking about the tectonics of building. It's about going back to the basis of how you form something," says Richard Serra. "I wanted to make these Torqued Ellipses, but nobody knew how to make them. I went to Korea, then Baltimore, where they ended up miscalculating the drawing. I figured out how to use line heat and oil to bring the steel plates together. Finally a friend found a plant in Germany that said they could make them. Germans take such pride in craftsmanship."

O, the mysterious origins of our art. I sip red wine from my Klean Kanteen. Adam jerks his crossed ankle nervously, while his chapped fingers crack each knuckle one by one. Part of my thesis at Cornell involved writing a poetics, or discourse on my work—an investigation of my thought processes, methods, some form of composition tying self-analysis to my own creativity. It was the hardest assignment I've ever had to do. It forced me to become a spectator. It severed me from my art.

I study Serra's mannerisms closely. To talk about the effect of your art constantly does something to an artist. Creates, in you, a character. A celebrity. Mounted to the wall behind them is an enlarged black and white photograph of Richard Serra close up, his eyes facing the camera—a piercing light gray, his name plastered in all CAPS beneath him.

You turn into an image of yourself.

"Thoughts and drawings work in order to portray a sequence of the evolution of things. Looking at a sculpture, you *recon-sider* it."

"And what kind of process does that involve?" Garrett asks. "Reconsidering a sculpture."

The Fifth Wall

I realize I haven't even seen the sculpture yet, completed. I've been completely avoiding the building.

Richard Serra looks slightly down past the audience, as if talking to the floor. "I call my sculptures 'Living Art.' It's about having a sense of understanding of the relationships between your body and its location. And not just in relations to other objects, but the spaces in between. The void is as interesting as material form."

The audience resonates a combination of contemplative "mmms" and agreeable "mm-hmms." Garrett continues to nod. Not once have the two, interviewer and interviewee, looked at one another. Adam, expressionless, stares intently at them. Something about him feels far away.

"It's like his answers are pre-prepared," I whisper. "His theory and methodology outlined in dotted lines."

"I think he's fucking genius," he mutters.

I take another swig.

"To experience a sculpture," says Garrett, "is then to connect with the piece physically. To accept it into your frame of reference as real, and thus allow it to play with space—to let it, essentially, trick you."

Richard Serra blinks, his expression unchanging. He continues as if reading from a script. He is fragile with his mannerisms, undoubtedly serene. "You start to question things such as, 'what does it mean to round a bend?' It's about looking at the whole— the *here* and the *void* simultaneously. Place in relation to time and space. It's a different way of remembering. You don't just see things; you see things amongst things."

The wine surges through my bloodstream. I find my eyes unable to fix onto one single object, my mind unable to concentrate on one single thing. What are we even doing here? I lean closer to Adam in order to feel his energy, trying to gauge his mood, but it's like he's behind a wall. I glance down at Mal's low-cut v-neck that I snatched from her laundry this morning to look sexy and make sure that nothing's popping out.

"One of my most precious memories is of watching three hyper children become completely quiet while experiencing a Torqued Ellipse." Richard Serra smiles. He shakes his head, laughs gently. "They stopped their shrieking, and kicking, and whining, and settled down into true receivers, real explorers of space. You see, kids have no preconceptions of art. They run through and immediately get lost in the piece. They're naturally inquisitive about space and the world around them. They don't care if it's *sculpture*." He yawns, takes a sip of water, rests his hand on his knee.

"What about the experience of *Band*? How would you describe it to the audience, for those who haven't experienced it, or who don't know what to think when perhaps overwhelmed by its structure?"

"The entire sheet of steel, as it undulates from the space, changes continuously, as does its interior and exterior. You can move outside the band continuously and never stop. You might have the concern that you're walking back in the same direction that you came from, but you're not. It's difficult to tell one space from the other; you sense that they're similar but they're all dissimilar. The sculpture creates new spaces in the architecture of the room."

Garrett announces that time has caught up with them, and thanks Richard Serra for the talk. The audience gives a round of applause. The artist nods politely, smiles with healthy teeth, and Garrett asks for volunteers for a brief Q and A.

"Before anybody asks it, the answer to the most predominant question I receive is—*No*, my sculptures are not *walls*."

The audience laughs, though I'm not sure why this is funny. Why couldn't the sculpture be a wall if it was the spectator's experience of a wall? Isn't that what his whole fucking lecture was about?

The Fifth Wall

Adam nudges me and nods toward the exit; I follow him—squeezing around knees and pointy shoes and up the aisle, through the main lobby, and outside into brisk air and a darkening city.

Adam lights up a cigarette. I watch him inhale it with his whole body, his skin absorbing its smoky gray sheen.

"No Q and A?" I lean against a railing.

Adam paces along the concrete. "Q and A's a joke. You know that."

"Is something wrong?"

He looks at me with that expression I recognize so suddenly that it hollows my stomach—that look of inexplicable inquiry, as if he's assessing my thought patterns, coding my emotions into a categorical script. It feels like there's a camera pointed at me. Neither of us says anything. Sirens resound in the distance, growing louder for a moment and then receding into muted echoes, mixing back in with the steady hum of downtown traffic. The wine pulls my brain in different directions. My ankles feel loose and wobbly. I watch a man whisper something into a woman's ear, her face expanding with each word until she bursts with a cackle.

Adam pulls a hard drag and tosses the butt on the ground; a thin line of smoke wavers up, disappearing into the atmosphere.

"I gotta go take a piss," he says.

I watch him disappear into the building.

Leaning against the railing quickly becomes uncomfortable, so I shift to standing, and suddenly I'm immersed in a pocket of cool air that sends shivers up my bare arms and neck. A new awareness enters—I feel naked in the space around me, feel the lack of action and purpose in my stance—my empty hands, having nothing to hold, drink, smoke . . . it's times like these when I sincerely wish I liked cigarettes, when every eye feels like its focused on me, every object becomes a witness to my inability to hold my own space, to gain control of the situation, to stand strong in the midst of some sort of belief system I'm supposed to have created just by being alive. But instead all my thoughts feel fraudulent, fickle, and insincere.

What the fuck is Adam's problem?

These past few weeks all I've wanted was to please him, to embody an image of this terrifying artist he projected onto me the moment we reunited in this very place—almost the exact space I'm standing right now, alone.

I burst through the main lobby and head towards the restrooms. I pace amongst a few groups of loitering, also anti-Q and A individuals discussing the lecture approvingly, or at least that's how it feels—like everyone in this materialist, multibillion-dollar hellhole adheres to a certain kind of "high art" discourse, fashions their opinions around a collective intellectualism defining what is and isn't *good* art. *Let me tell you something*—I hear my father's famous phrase activate my stream of thoughts—*the way you look at me, Adam, feels like a knife being plunged into the essence of my being—the way you push and pull and always have, finding glimpses of some part of yourself in me you feel you've lost, and the second I rebel from that image you fucking cowardly turn away.*

A dark figure swishes in my sight's periphery and I catch the back of Adam's jacket vanishing through the exit door to the side staircase, leading to the lower atrium.

Where the fuck is he going?

I dart behind him, following his quick footsteps down the stairs and emerge into the atrium housing the massive, slithering *Band*. The sculpture towers above the ground, a magnificent fluid ribbon. "Adam?" I call out, spotting a dark body wind around the gleaming orange edge. I follow the echoes of his movement, running my fingers along the cold steel surface of its flawless curvature, each piece mathematically constructed to balance atop one another without welding, as if steel were a durable material you could mold with your hands. "Adam?" I call out again. The tapping of his boots echo on the concrete; they resound with what sounds like the opposite side of the sculpture, but from all the echoing, it's difficult to really tell. I continue to move along the contorting wall, experiencing the changes in space that the steel structure provokes, becoming lost along its labyrinthine body, the ground feeling no longer fixed. *You might have the concern that you're walking back in the same direction that you came from, but you're not...*

"I thought it might be you."

Startled, I whip around to the voice—a tall, gangly body mimicking my gesture along the steel surface with his hand, his face enveloped in the shadow of the sculpture's curve. "How did you..." I look behind me and then back at him. He slides towards me along the metal as I walk backwards, his face now coming into the light.

"How did I what?"

"Oh my God—," I jump back, cupping my hands to my mouth. The artist Michael Landy grins wide. I start to nervously giggle. Have I been following Michael Landy this whole fucking time?

"I haven't seen you in ages. I'd planned to run into you, but you seemed to just vanish like the Drog."

"Well here I am, *coincidentally*," I pause, "right back where I started."

"Ah," Michael Landy smiles. "So you heard."

"The basics," I say, continuing to look around for Adam as we move incrementally along the sculpture. I really could have sworn it was him. "Did you figure out the problem?"

Adam's uncanny clone shrugs. "Something happened in the wiring—to be frank, we're not exactly sure. I had to dismantle him. My partners shipped another prototype from L.A.—a smaller version, one of the earlier models. It's not as exciting, but it'll have to do. It's still, you know, press."

"A human error in the end then, I suppose."

He stares at me intensely. "We are human because we're defective."

"What are you doing down here anyway?" I nearly shout at him, feeling overwhelmed and flustered, pulsating with built-up adrenaline for a confrontation with another man.

He eyes me mischievously. "I came to get some air, some space to think. There's something about being in the presence of a great object that has no other purpose but to *be*. It balances the advanced circuitry of the brain, don't you think?"

I stare at him. Around a curve we bend and dip, absorbed in the sculpture's imposing utterance—I take it all in, feeling this grand presence of icy steel in my bones.

"There's something about you." In the light, Michael Landy looks worn out and haggard, his dark eyes reflecting off the sculpture in a glowing orange-red.

"Oh?"

"Something charged. Something desperate. Something wild. I'm very sensitive to energies. Often I can see auras. Yours—," he reaches his hand towards me, squinting his eyes, "—*ah*, precisely…yours is a luminous red." An enormous grin spreads across his face. Loose curls fall against his forehead. "Red, the life-blood force. The color of survival, action, anger, and love—of *revolution*."

"Are you sure it's not just the reflection of the sculpture?"

"I felt it the day I met you. It drew me towards you. This compelling energy. Very masculine, and yet exceedingly sexual."

He shifts closer to me, his face now only a few inches from mine, and I stare up at this bizarre creature—his expression gleaming, pulsating, alive with a similar sort of energy that he just described, though terribly invasive.

"What are you so afraid of?" he whispers.

His question echoes deep into my body, penetrates my every cell. We inch around *Band*'s curves like slinking centipedes, shadowed and unshadowed in its slick, sweeping metal. Whether it's the alcohol, my depression, or the presence of some invigorating aura—I feel gripped with a racing terror. I rush to check and see if Adam's called or texted, but the screen is black and dead; recently it's been doing that, dying suddenly, even if nearly fully charged. I feel like slamming it against the wall.

"Hey, let's say we get out of here—?" Skin brushes my wrist.

"Have you eaten yet?"

My focus switches to my stomach, and I register that I haven't ingested much all day besides some Ritz crackers and bland cheese before the lecture, and a bottle of cheap Zinfandel. I shake my head, feeling the hollow in my stomach.

And he's calling an Uber. He's leading me up the staircase towards a terrifying city. He's saying he knows a hidden gem with the best dumpling soup in town, close to the Airbnb he's been renting in Chinatown—evidence that he does, in fact, leave the museum. But now we're stopping in the stairwell; he's frantically searching through his pockets. He's pulling out a tiny plastic baggie filled with a fine, snow-white powder. *I hope you don't mind,* he is saying, *I've also invited my dear friend, Molly.* His grin is like the Cheshire's. He's inserting the tip of a key into the powder and thrusting it up into his right nostril, inhaling grotesquely, rubbing the excess powder around both nostril cavities. Something about his smile feels artificial, infected— as if masking a great dread that permeates this scene. But the temptation intensifies the second I see his body shudder gratifyingly, lights a burning ember in my chest. I lick my finger and dip it into the bag, then shove it in my mouth, cringing from the bitter, acidic taste.

But where is Adam?

"This is the purest of the pure," Michael Landy is saying. "None of that rat poison bullshit. This is Silk Road pure—the finest MDMA Bitcoin can buy!"

Almost instantly I feel my awareness changing, my body tingling, my chest opening up in a massive fluttering, the setting around me pulsating with new waves and flows, the darkness in my perception altering—a new aura of possibility. Michael Landy's face glows with near-deafening charisma; I feel his fierce energy all over me.

Fuck Adam Black.

What *am* I so afraid of?

The restaurant is crowded and bustling; a young waiter runs back and forth between packed tables—obviously the owner's offspring or some close relation—while two women manning the register also rush steaming food from the small kitchen window to random tables in what appears to be no logical or working system—just pure, gastronomic chaos. The lighting surrounds us with a harsh yellow; the smells of bone broth, fried meats, over-steeped green tea, fresh white rice. Metal silverware clinks on water glasses and ceramic plates; paper placemats dampen and tear from watermarks; wooden chopsticks scrape together. I stare at my humongous bowl of bulbous dumplings floating in a thick, oily broth with deafening, over-joyous hunger. A tall frozen glass of Singha tastes refreshing after the heat of soup; Michael Landy orders more cool, cloudy sake for the table. Hot and cold, hot and cold. I feel charged with what feels like a heavy light—not a lightness that's peaceful, but feels directive, and all-consuming—as if controlling my perception with a heavy, monstrous hand.

"What I love about Chinatown," Landy chews and talks, "is how it feels like it's its own separate world. A different culture, a different language, a different pace—like it's somehow severed from real time, existing alongside of it! I feel a great—," he conjures with his hands, takes a deep breath, closes his eyes, inhales, "—presence in this community—something deep and lurking beneath the bustling city streets, behind these run-down store fronts and trash-filled alleyways—like a three-headed dragon asleep for thousands of years, hidden below concrete, just waiting to be jarred awake." He looks around suspiciously, eyes widening.

Behind us, the door to the restaurant opens and closes, cool air coming and going, the constant ringing of a bell.

I find myself nodding crazily. "Perhaps that's what's causing all the earthquakes. A dragon rustling beneath San Francisco, stirring in his sleep."

Michael Landy smiles. "Just imagine this city reacting to a disaster on that kind of level."

"The dragon level?"

We both crack up.

"I expect we'd do exactly what New York did in the aftermath of September 11th," he says.

"Which was what?"

"Call Hollywood, obviously."

"Shut the fuck up."

"But doesn't it make the most sense? Who else in this country has experience with disasters on that type of a scale?"

I tell him about the real government webpage for the Zombie Apocalypse that Mal showed me the other day, with literal steps and courses of action on how to proceed in case of emergency. How it exists, seriously, without any irony or self-reference to its own fiction.

"Propaganda!" Michael Landy downs a shot of sake and waves me off.

Clatters and clinks resound in the restaurant in jarring patterns. I feel the weight of zealous consumption surrounding us—humans reduced to grotesque creatures, mouths buried in bowls, slurping questionably sourced ingredients, screeching in harsh, drawn-out vowels—the pure noises and sounds of the living.

"What's more interesting to me are *drones*," Michael Landy is saying. "All of a sudden *drones* are everywhere—shipping our packages, filming aerial porn in epic landscapes, flooding social media like a virus. It's hilarious!"

"Why is it hilarious?"

He guffaws. "I'm surprised at you. Don't tell me you haven't spotted the most textbook example of blatant propaganda!"

I shake my head.

Michael Landy exaggerates a loud sigh. *"Obviously* it's all a ploy to acclimate Americans to drone flights over civilian territory."

A catchy rap song immediately enters my brain. *"That drone cool, but I hate that drone—chocolate chip cookie dough in a sugar cone. Drones in the morning, drones in the night. I'm trying to find a pretty drone to take home tonight."* I tap my fingers on my leg to the beat, though I can't seem to synchronize the two properly.

"You know, this is all precisely what the Drog plays on," he's saying, "—using this feared war technology to create an instrument that *sees* and *feels* without actually seeing and feeling. The interactive social experiment becomes how the viewers respond to the machine's assessment of them—an assessment way beyond the powers of our natural senses. It produces real terror and fear."

I glare at him. "You planned the whole escape scenario, didn't you?"

"I didn't say that."

"Then how else does a machine just *disappear* and somehow avoid all the security cameras? Where was it hiding? And how did it end up exactly where it started?" I feel my hands shaking, my teeth grinding, my brain moving a mile a minute. "There's no other logical explanation."

"Why, there's violence merely in the Drog's existence. You have to remember that this isn't a new invention—the model that it's replicated from has existed for more than a few years now. Its usage in the military is publically documented in both Iraq and Afghanistan. My mere gesture of copying it and displaying it in a prestigious museum for others to look at as art is in itself a very violent action."

"It's contributing to its propaganda."

Michael Landy clasps his hands together. "That's exactly what it's doing. It's revealing and mimicking the whole concept, but outlandishly so. What happened in the museum—when the Drog escaped—was merely a coincidence, but a coincidence of the highest order. An effect that I couldn't have planned better if I tried. The machine came alive in a way I've never seen before. In a way that I, or anyone at my company, has yet to understand. But the moment when coincidences start to happen, a whole new world opens up, and if you look closely—take them as signs—only then can you see what the world at large has to offer."

I stare at him.

"We *willed* the Drog to escape, is what I'm trying to say, Sheila. It manifested our deepest desires!"

I think about that awfully sunny day just over three months ago when I walked Mal's bike up the inclined driveway, along the cobblestone pathway to the door. I propped the bike on my shoulder, I opened the front glass door. I pushed in the wooden door. I watched my mother pull the trigger.

Did I will it to happen? The pull I'd felt was definitely real— the strong desire to come home. Would it have happened if I hadn't bought the ticket? If I'd decided to call first to let her know I was coming, to let her know that I was there?

"There's nothing more relevant today than fear." Michael Landy pours us each more sake to the brim of our minuscule glasses. His mouth seems to be moving at a speed faster than his voice. "Most of us don't even realize that we live with this ever-constant notion of doom—we all subconsciously know that we've extended the resources of our planet well beyond their possible usages. Fear is a response that's been preserved throughout evolution—working up to this very point in time for its optimal usefulness. It's only a matter of time now, with more and more cancers, ecological disasters, the ticking clock of nuclear weapons..."

Earlier this morning I'd been listening to a podcast about how in Pakistan, they shuttle their nukes from station to station in, quite literally, trucks on the streets. How right now a band of lunatics could be hijacking the world's most powerful and deathly weapons. A nuclear bomb could go off at any moment, but for some reason we're not talking about this all the time. We don't seem to be doing anything.

"I think we crave it, this fear," I'm saying to him. "We crave it without even knowing it. And this feels like the scariest part."

"Well sure, we want fear—its thrill, its stimulation—but without its consequences, of course. The excitement of danger without the danger itself. That's the American way! And it's simply the best way to employ a system of power."

"But fear drives people to do horrible things..." My eyes feel like they're popping out of my skull.

"It's when the desire to *live* kicks in, Sheila. Where do you think all this technology comes from? *Fear of death.* The ultimate fear. What *The Last Art* is all about! Our fear has brought us to the point where we're quite literally transcending our limitations, well on our way to becoming—well—dare I say, *Gods?* I mean, why do you think 'superfoods' are becoming so popular? We're preparing our bodies to go up into space! Technology has become a secondary force of evolution—we've successfully combined our thumbs with our brains to the point where we're manifesting our imaginations, reverse-engineering life. Artificial systems are behaving more and more like natural systems—we're finding the patterns in brain waves to match up with the layouts of city structures, which matches up with the physical structures of microscopic bacterium, which matches up with fucking *dark matter*...these coincidences aren't accidents."

I slam my hand down on the table. "But what if the coincidences are excruciating?" I nearly yell at him. "What if the 'whole new world' that opens up is one that's terrifying and nightmarish? Where all the signs feel deceptive, unwelcome—*punishing* for no apparent reason?"

Michael Landy's smile is serpentine. He runs his fingers through his silky curls and leans forward. "Then obviously they're tests."

"Of *what*?"

"Why, character, of course. You must understand your given role before you can move forward in this grand play."

Immediately this whole scene feels distinctly familiar—not that I've been here before, but that I've felt exactly this way. The movement in the restaurant begins to slow down as parts. I take in the setting around me as if in a series of slow-motion shots. The jiggling skin of the stocky food runner as she throttles forward. The jingling of the front door. The scrape of a metal spoon against ceramic. Michael Landy's mouth contorting without sound, the contours in his face offering a slightly more grotesque version of Adam's, *off* in just a way that haunts every expression, intensifies every word. The world around me begins to flicker like a faulty image in a film; I see my mother with her head split open on the floor, swelling and expanding dimensions, existing before me like a place; it fills up my brain like the closing in of a camera on a face. Like Andy Warhol's screen tests; *The Passion of Joan of Arc*. It chokes the entire screen. The Lack, I recognize all too well—but this time I carefully observe it, allow myself to stay floating outside of it. I feel rage forming, confusion, near debilitating grief. The emotions arrive one after another in almost perfect succession—building, building—overwhelming my exterior reality, as if turning me inside out.

Like a tumor, attacking from the inside, and watching the body fall. I'm turning imagination against itself, provoking my own psychotic state, triggering my nervous system to self-destruct.

Rachel Nagelberg

Everything around me begins to swell. The windows disappear. The walls fall away. The floor becomes merely a plain to stay afloat.

Outside the moon is a screaming bright orifice and the air is alive in millions of chilling waves. We tear through pulsating, claustrophobic streets, packed with bodies clutching shopping bags, shrieking children, arms shoving restaurant fliers in faces, hunched old ladies pushing through crowds, bent over in markets picking through dried crustaceans emanating harrowing scents of the shriveling, of the dead. Lit Chinese lanterns in greens, yellows, and reds drape from streetlights and buildings, crisscrossing above us in an ethereal glow. Crowds accumulate weight at red-lighted crosswalks, form a mass of one deep, holding breath, before the light hits green and it bursts.

"Click your heels and follow me," Michael Landy is saying. His hands are flailing in wild gestures as he talks. We pass by stores with huge glass displays showcasing colorful figurines, golden moving cat sculptures, jade dragons, thousands of loose tinned teas. My shoulders brush against other shoulders and arms, my teeth clenching and unclenching, my brain a soaring, swollen balloon.

We break through the masses and wind around a side street into a calmer darkness lit in pale yellow light, the sounds of crowds now hollow and retreating into the distance. We wind around a few more constricted, dark streets, the whole time Michael Landy grasping my hand and swinging it—our motions like Hansel and Gretel, naively walking along on the path to our own doom.

We come upon a dark, cavernous entrance below an unlit marquee.

"Are you ready to embark on a journey?"

I push him. "You're not going to take me into this abandoned theater and murder me, are you?"

The Fifth Wall

He laughs, and leads me to the ticket booth. "We're going to a show."

I watch him approach a dark, closed window. "Is this some kind of joke?"

He looks back at me, his eye catching the glimmer of a streetlight above.

A shuffling from the ticket booth. I jump back. A tiny red light appears. A soft woman's voice.

"Two to The Lost Theater," says Michael Landy. I approach the booth cautiously, examining the petite woman inside sporting a 1920s updo hairstyle and dark red lipstick. She sizes me up with a snarling grin, checks something off on a list. "You may enter," she says.

"*The Lost Theater?*" I whisper to Michael Landy as we walk towards the dark entrance. "What's the *The Lost Theater?*"

He squeezes my hand and tells me to come along. We enter through an open glass door and follow what I now notice is a crimson red carpet—lit from along the sides of the floor in dim golden lighting. The building itself is airy and high-ceilinged and vast; lining the walls are empty poster display cases doused in graffiti. Lingering scents of dust and mold.

Sounds begin to emanate from behind two approaching closed doors, outlined from behind in a glowing red. A floor standing sign reads *Welcome to the Underworld* in printed golden script. Michael Landy pushes open the doors.

Madness. We enter into an enormous theater alive with flashing bodies, colors, and music, the red carpet beneath us like a long tongue expanding down between the seats to a grand, open stage. Glass chandeliers dangle from the ceiling lit with electric copper-colored lights. I stand gaping as a bikini-ed aerial acrobat dangles on stage from flowing silk lavender ribbons, contorting her body in swift, balletic movements. Below her, a pianist dressed in a full-piece suit plays jazz on a grand piano, the tails of his jacket fluttering along with his movement as people gather around him, a few couples dancing. Tall women dressed in sequined one-pieces and feather headdresses swish by us, holding glasses of champagne, laughing. A waiter offers us some sort of fresh fish hors d'oeuvre off a round silver tray. I shake my head no, still shocked by the reality of the scene. Groups of people cluster about the theater, some seated in the audience, others gathered on tufted sofas and chairs arranged below the stage. Everyone seems to be dressed in elaborate costume, faces gleaming with makeup. Men in high heels wearing sparkling thongs with suspenders; bodies in fluorescent wigs, doused with glitter. Michael Landy grasps my shoulder, shaking me. "Wake up, Sheila." He's laughing now, loving the expression on my face, so blissfully entertained.

"I don't think I'm dressed for this," I mutter.

"Nonsense!" He leads me up a side staircase to the mezzanine, which has been converted into a full bar and lounge. Small round tables line the outer edges of the balcony, which is itself aligned with leather booths and vintage looking velour furniture—the original box seating having been gutted and restored to a gleaming hardwood floor. Candles on the tables create a mysterious, romantic glow, lighting up people's faces with shadows like masks.

We brush by bodies adorned with furs and pearls, others sporting shimmering antlers, tails, and whiskers, over to a seated sharp-looking older man dressed in a silver pinstripe three-piece suit, his sleek silver hair gelled back like a movie star's, puffing from a long electric cigarette. Next to him a nude woman painted from head to toe in leopard print sips from a clear martini, two cats ears poking out from her spiraling black curls. On his other side, a thin man in a dark green suit and a waxed mustache scribbles in a small spiral notebook, sips bourbon from an ornate glass tumbler.

"Landy!" The silver-haired man looks up, his voice surprisingly high and effeminate. "What the fuck are you doing here?"

The Fifth Wall

"Eli Moscowitz, the devil himself."

Eli stands up and the two shake hands, Eli grinning with bulging eyes, dark black eyeliner. "I hear you're working on a big show, you motherfucker. Good for you. This guy," Eli looks at me, "pure fucking genius," he points. He sits back down in the booth, crosses his legs, takes a puff of his e-cigarette. He shouts to the bartender to fix us some drinks. "As you can see," Eli holds out his hands, "it's a pretty big production now." Eli talks loud at Landy, his voice oddly like a teenager's in the body of an androgynous mobster.

Michael Landy nods. "It's totally *alive*."

Eli grins, a golden tooth catching the light with a blinding gleam.

"How do you two know each other?" I ask.

"It doesn't fucking matter how we know each other," barks Eli. "I don't give a fuck about how you know anyone." He laughs, vapor escaping from his lips. The leopard caresses his leg, her eyes fixated on me mischievously. The scribbling waxed mustache man smirks. "All that matters is who you are, right now, in this theater."

Who the fuck is this guy? I mouth the words to Michael Landy, who, grinning, just winks at me, then holds out his hand in a gesture as if to say *just settle down, wait and see.*

A waiter sets down our drinks. The leopard leans in to Eli's neck and lightly bites him, causing Eli to turn to her with a lustful force; she unscrews the top of a pendant from a necklace camouflaged in the paint around her neck, and holds up a tiny silver spoon to Eli's nostril. He violently snorts the white bumps, first in his left nostril, and then in his right, thrusts his head back, wiggles furiously, whoops with energy. "Mercury was just telling us about her experience *suspending*," he talks rapidly. "You know— hanging on a rig from those fucking metal hooks in your skin."

"He, like, thinks it's another form of *theater*," says Mercury, the leopard, screwing back together the pendant.

Rachel Nagelberg

"He thinks *everything*'s a form of theater," says Waxed Mustache.

"It's a living *confrontation*, a superior act of *concentration*—a massive focus of a large group." Eli flicks his wrist. "Describe the grotesque fucking thing, sweetheart."

"I was, like, hanging from four hooks—two in my shoulder blades and two in the sides of my knees," Mercury gestures a motion of floating with her hands, "and I was like, raised above this guy who was suspended below me, but facing up—and we were staring into one another during this crazy intimate experience with, like, drums playing and the whole group seated Indian style surrounding us, chanting in an ancient language. It was, like, the pain was a button that blasted us off into this other dimension. It was so much more than, like, having sex. We couldn't even have sex afterward—sex was like, *nothing* compared to that kind of intimacy. We were totally lost in it." She turns towards Eli. "It was *fucking insane*," she mouths the words seductively at him. He stares at her wildly, ripples of energy pulsating through him, cobalt veins bulging in his neck.

"I think I want to do this," his manic, effeminate voice is saying. "This fucking cat here is selling it *hard*." He laughs furiously.

"My roommate sometimes hosts them in our backyard," says Waxed Mustache. "I'll definitely let you know when the next one's happening."

"No, no," Eli shakes his head aggressively. "We need to get it in *here*. We need to bring it to the *theater*—get my drift?"

"Totally," Mustache says. "Oh man, dude, *yes*."

Michael Landy scoffs. "It's *Modern Primitivism*, Eli. It's a cultural fashion show."

"It's like, *so* much more than that."

"Yeah, Landy, don't knock it 'til you try it!"

"Oh, I'm not *knocking* it at all. I think it's a decidedly spiritual act. I'm merely pointing out that *flesh hook suspension* began

154

as a rite of passage in the Mandan tribe in the early eighteen hundreds—"

"Here we go with the *Landyisms*."

"—and that this kind of 'suspension' *lacks* the whole ritualistic part. Just think about it—the act itself of literally inserting hooks systematically on certain points of the body naturally causes the release of endorphins, adrenaline, fight or flight responses, which will immediately cause one to perhaps *believe* what they imagine the definition of transcending to be."

I nod. "You know after the great performance artist Stelarc suspended himself between skyscrapers, he wrote that he no longer needed his mind to understand the immense pain that overcame his body. He called his body *the zombie body*."

"Or *the body without organs*," says Michael Landy, quoting Deleuze and Guattari.

"He said he understood its 'total obsolescence,'" I continue, "—it wasn't about *transcending*, it was really about metaphorically suspending yourself in a non-place between mind and body, past and future—he said it was torturous."

"It's *shamanic*," Mercury protests. "The ritual *is* the act. Don't tell me you're one of those people who believes that culture can't exist in modernity."

"You fucks can intellectualize it all you want," barks Eli. "But unless you've actually tried it, your opinion is pretty much null."

"I've, like, honestly never had an experience that was *more* intimate."

"Oh, come *on*." Michael Landy throws up his hands and points at Mercury. "You were looking for a thrill, an *experience*, an *escape*. You wanted to fuck that guy, and in order to do that, you were willing to stick a thick, cold piece of sharp metal under your skin and *have that experience*. I have to hand it to you—that takes real balls."

Eli smacks his hand on his lap, bawling from laughter. "Now

this is entertainment," he shrieks. Mercury grabs Eli's e-cigarette and puffs it, rolling her eyes.

"And of *course* the sex was bad," adds Michael Landy, smirking. "It would have been, anyway. The suspension just gave you both the perfect excuse."

I sit sipping my drink amidst a body chaos, aware of the dilation of my pupils, the chemicals rushing through my veins. "I think really everything just boils down to comfort and discomfort," I find myself saying. "It's the human condition—the nature of having bodies." I look around, still trying to place myself, feeling the incredible discomfort in my own body—its inability to align with my racing mind, resisting the electrifying MDMA, my voice sounding foreign and disassociated in this loud, pulsating room. "Where the fuck are we anyway?" I say loudly. "What even *is* this place?"

Eli stops laughing and looks at me sharply. Michael Landy reveals sparkling teeth.

"Fresh meat," says Waxed Mustache.

Mercury, grinning, narrows her gaze.

Eli snaps his fingers up high, signaling for more drinks. He cracks his neck from side to side, then fixates his gaze directly on me.

"Welcome to your fucking show," he says.

I stare at him. "What do you mean *my* show?"

Michael Landy clasps his hands together, giddy with excitement, nearly jumping out of his seat. Eli laughs, vapor escaping from his lips. A waiter sets down fresh drinks. I sip my drink—the slosh of creamy, bitter whiskey. Jazz piano mixes with ambient undertones spurting from hidden speakers, red lights flashing, the mezzanine whirls.

"*Obviously* you've never before been more in need of a theater."

"What do you—"

"THIS, here, is *culture*." Eli's eyes widen—two dark orbs

The Fifth Wall

surrounded by thick black outlining. "The real essence of San Francisco *boiled down* to its thick, gritty remnants—and *digested* into a living performance that never stops."

He slams his hand on the table. The room spins. *"And what do you mean it never stops?"* He interrupts my thought process. "I see this question on your fucking face. A person who even *thinks* this idiotic question must still believe in such things as *ends*. But here there is no beginning and there's never an end; *the show* is constantly happening all around us."

"She, like, still believes in an *outside*," says Mercury.

"An outside to *what?*" I stammer.

Mercury unscrews the lid to her necklace and holds up a bump for Eli, who snorts with a tremendous force. "DRINK ME says the tiny bottle on the table," he shouts, "EAT ME says the cake! We must ingest substances that alter our consciousnesses, release chemicals into our brains; we must shift the *Now* into a more comfortable and pliable form."

"Perception is, like, everything." She takes a bump herself. The whole room feels like it's shaking.

"Too much art today exists *outside* of life." Eli's limbs flail. "Art as a *concept*, art as an *institution*—you fucking *intellectual* fucks. It's CONSCIOUSNESS that's the highest form of art. Never has the artist been more in need of a *people*. Tell me you can't feel it in the vibrations in these *walls*—The Lost Theater is an operation of *death*. This theater is dying. Its walls are literally crumbling. Our bodies are dying. Everything in this space is dying. The only thing that's alive here is *the show*."

The theater flickers in and out. I watch as Michael Landy dips his finger into the tiny bag, licks it monstrously. The glint of his crooked teeth. The noise in the room like a deafening hollow of sharp consonants and static.

"Your inner monologue is dying to be spoken. I see it writhing on your fucking, twisted face. I feel it in your manic energy."

"You can see it in her blood red aura," adds Michael Landy.

157

"Your LIFE feels like a SERIES of ACTS, DOESN'T IT?" Eli is shrieking amidst the chaos. "LIKE EVERY MINUTE AND SECOND ARE PERFECTLY TIMED, WHERE EVERY LINE SPOKEN TO YOU AND FROM YOU FEELS PURPOSEFUL AND RELEVANT, LIKE IT'S ALL CONTRIBUTING TO SOMETHING LARGER THAT YOU KNOW IS THERE—YOU CAN FUCKING FEEL IT CONSTANTLY—BUT IT FEELS JUST OUT OF REACH..."

"Yes," I'm nodding. "Yes." The voice emanating from my mouth feels distant and strange. Tears are streaming down my face. My heart feels as if it's ballooning out into the crevices of my ribs, forcing them to their skeletal limit.

"Tell me something," Waxed Mustache says to me as he scribbles, "what kind of *role* do you see playing in your own life?"

"Yes, like—what kind of *experience* are you, like, looking to have?"

Michael Landy's bloodshot eyes glimmer in the distance.

Eli leans in quietly. The whole room pauses, as if a film on a screen. His eyes are penetrating, devilish. "Tell me," he whispers, "do you think of yourself as doomed?"

CLOSE ON SHEILA as she stands up, staggers backwards away from table. CONTRAZOOM as SHEILA begins to reevaluate the scene: CLOSE UPs on faces more clearly—the pale, sickly gray quality to WAXED MUSTACHE's face; ELI's facial stubble, eyeliner running, slobber all over his suit jacket, watching him nearly fall over, so high he can hardly sit up; MERCURY's smudged leopard paint, cracked dry lips; MICHAEL LANDY's bloodshot eyes, his wicked smile.

FLASH CUTS to previously seen people in theater but now with gaudy make-up that's dried, cracked, and smudged; eyes blazed; wrinkles in skin; bloated

The Fifth Wall

bellies. The AERIAL DANCER's bulging veins. An UNAT-
TRACTIVE MAN wearing a monocle grotesquely squeezing
a DANCER's exposed breast; a CLOSE UP of him licking
her dark, engorged nipple.

MICHAEL LANDY approaches SHEILA as she backs away
in horror. He motions to her in elaborate gestures,
his face contorting into monstrous expressions (MIT
OUT SOUNDS of his voice so she's only hearing her
own internal TRACK of theater's confused chaotic
noises). MICHAEL LANDY tries to grasp SHEILA, but
she pushes him away.

                    SHEILA
                  (shrieking)
             You're all fucking
             imposters!

The SOUND of an AUDIENCE laugh track.

                    SHEILA
             You think you're *artists*—but
             you're all just actors!

                     ELI
                  (laughing)
             You still think that your
             fucking art comes from *you*.
             Can't you see that you're
             just a filter? A vessel for
             the 'art' to flow through.
                  (pointing)
             You're the fucking imposter,

and you've known it all
along.

> SHEILA
> (squeezing the sides of her head)
> Some things have to be *real*.
> All this is *real*, isn't it?
> This is *actually happening*.

SHEILA has the urge to tap her feet together three times.

> MICHAEL LANDY
> We can choose the ways we
> want to live.
> (snorts from Mercury's
> necklace)
> But of course there's always
> a risk involved.

> MERCURY
> The risk is the fun part.

> WAXED MUSTACHE
> (scribbling)
> Now, if you could be *anyone*,
> who would you choose?

> SHEILA
> (wildly)
> How am I supposed to play a
> role when I can't even play
> the role of myself?

The Fifth Wall

ELI

This is the *magic* of this
city—a city of mirrors. The
trick is when you think you're
lost, you're actually always
there, right fucking in front
of yourself.

SHEILA
(nearly pulling out her
hair)
(to MICHAEL LANDY)

I didn't *will* it to happen.
I never *wanted* it to happen.
I walked in the door and
there she was. It was a
split second and then she
pulled the trigger. What
kind of world produces that
kind of *coincidence?* What
kind of world hands me that
kind of *guilt?*

I collapse into my seat, feel myself back in my living body, my
whole being heaving with breath. I find myself telling the table
my story—how I felt a pull to fly back west—like a ghost calling
out to me, the future sending me a message. I tell it exactly
like it happened. How I rode Mal's bicycle up to the door, how
I opened it and saw her pull the trigger. How the bike fell on
top of me in this horrific moment, interrupting my processing,
causing me to fall. Eli and Mercury listen intently, eyes widening as I continue my tale. Michael Landy nods—almost satisfyingly—while Waxed Mustache, enthralled, twirls his mustache.
I tell them about the discovered brain tumor, and then about

the deconstruction and the camera. How it all came to me as if in a nightmare in which I never awoke. How I've been having these moments in my life where I completely lose myself in my own trauma and act without knowing or remembering—how I've nicknamed them *the Lacks*. How I've never been able to say what actually happened out loud; I've been holding the truth in, grasping onto it for dear life, attracting violence everywhere, waiting for someone to save me.

"This is fascinating," says Eli.

"It's *brilliant*," says Mercury.

"This is in Berkeley, you say?" asks Michael Landy.

I nod. Eli's eyes widen. He downs the rest of his drink and slams it on the table.

"The party bus!" he shouts, nearly choking. "Where the fuck is Rudolf?"

Mercury puffs the e-cigarette. "He's probably out back smoking a bowl."

I look at my phone to check the time, and then remember that it died hours ago.

And we're gliding downstairs, my arm being pulled by Eli, the sour smell of sweat and whiskey, charging through the masses—the drugged out dancers, the costumed audience. By now the magic of the room is dwindling; the pianist has his pants off, is bent down beneath the whip of a pudgy dominatrix while a small crowd gathers around. There's a DJ on the stage now, bodies before him writhing, pulsating, in blinking electric blue and white lights. They look like they could be holograms. Eli leads us to a side door, where we're stepping out into the dark, cavernous night. The outside air, a cool whip on my face and shoulders. The rumbling of an engine. We're climbing on a school bus painted in swirling colors, a mural depicting thousands of eyes.

"What's the address, Sweetheart?"

And I'm giving directions to a shaggy, meth-addict-looking man named Rudolf in the driver's seat. I'm being pulled into

The Fifth Wall

the gutted monstrosity on wheels, its floor layered in velour carpeting, aligned with polyester pillows, faux-fur blankets, strings of Christmas lights, a swirling disco ball.

Bump snort gag cough sniff trickle roar screech pan gurgle shriek laughter. Shadows immerse us. Bumpily we traverse overhangs, zoom through yellow lights. Like stage actors awaiting a performance in the wings; time becomes liminal, our mild conversation extraneous. Crossing the Bay Bridge feels like one great pause. A behind-the-scenes non-moment. Fingers and limbs everywhere. Bodily functions exaggerated; consumption, consumption. Higher and higher and—resume.

The bus with a thousand eyes pulls up to Ground Zero with an abrupt halt; the screech of the emergency brake; the heavy sigh of the door clutch releasing. We all stumble down its stairs, nearly falling out onto the dirt that meets the road. Eli whoops with energy; Mercury howls at a brilliant full moon. "Could there be a more *perfect* night for this?" she screams.

Rudolf sulks against the bus, lights a cigarette. "Am I fucking missing something?"

The street is dark and deathly quiet, the only light from a dim streetlight and a porch a few properties away, with faint sounds of our footsteps echoing, the movement of trees, the rustling of bushes, unseen animals scurrying, lemons falling from branches.

"There's the camera!" Waxed Mustache points excitedly, and the group follows his lead. We stand over the mounted device, now covered in a thick layer of dust and dirt—Eli and Mercury *oohing* and *ahhing*—as if examining artifacts in a ruin from an ancient civilization.

"Okay, *okay*," Eli staggers to the middle of the plot, Mercury following behind him in a sheer purple robe. "Here—you be Sheila." He flicks his wrist, motioning for her to retreat back to the start of the nonexistent path. "I'll be the Mother." Eli tries to balance but it appears increasingly hard for him to stand still without swaying; he keeps wiping away snot and drool from his face, his suit a wrinkled and dirty mess. "*LISTEN UP,*" he shrieks. A dog barks in the background, echoes in the gaping stillness. "*SHEILA ARE YOU LISTENING TO ME?*" Michael Landy and I approach the invisible stage they've created and plop down a few yards in front of them as the audience. I find that I am tongue-tied, and pinching myself, but I don't seem to be feeling any pain. Behind us, Waxed Mustache inspects the camera, mumbling to himself about the year and the make, furiously scribbling who-knows-what into his notebook. "This thing is on, right?"

"*THE EARTH IS A TEMPLE OF DEATH AND THE DYING.*" Eli dramatically cups his forehead. "*I WAS GIFTED A BRAIN TUMOR TO END THE ILLUSION OF A MERCIFUL GOD.*"

Off to the side, Mercury claps her hands together, squealing with delight, jumping up and down, barefoot on the dry, rough dirt, her feet cracked and bleeding.

I literally have no words for what's happening—my head still a churning mixture of substances, my body a physical confusion of sentiments.

As if given some cue, Mercury begins walking towards Eli, swaying her painted hips, thrusting her chest forward, feigning the motion of rolling a bicycle down an imaginary front path— meanwhile Eli paces around, expressing mixed emotions of consternation, misery, and terror on his face.

"*I'm going to surprise my mother,*" Mercury half-sings in her purple cape, like Little Red Riding Hood in a film adapted to an NC-17 porno.

"Why are they doing this?" I manage to whisper to Michael Landy, who grips my hand tightly and holds it against his chest.

"It looks like they're reenacting it so that you don't have to."

"*WHO AM I?*" Eli is screaming. "*NOW THAT MY BRAIN IS*

The Fifth Wall

BEING INVADED. *DO I LET IT TAKE ME, OR DO I TAKE MYSELF FIRST?"*

Mercury opens the invisible door on the invisible wall to the invisible house. Eli shoots himself in the head with his hand, feigns falling to the ground, aggressively twitching before lying still. Mercury gasps, then falls over herself, landing on Eli with the terrifying sound of dead weight. A moment of deep silence passes. Then Mercury lets out an enormous burp and they burst into a fit of hysterics, Eli wailing with laughter, clutching his stomach.

"Curtain!" he shrieks through the laughter. "Curtain!"

"These people are sickening." I say. "You people are fucking *sick!*" I scream.

The creaking of a door, footsteps on concrete. "I'm calling the police!" A neighbor shouts.

"FUCK YOU!" I scream back, now standing up and pacing back and forth.

Eli's doubled-over, trying to stand up, attempting to calm himself and Mercury from their drugged-out giddiness. "Let's fucking bolt," he staggers, "—but wait," he pauses, unzips his pants, barely getting his flaccid penis out before he starts pissing on the ruin.

Michael Landy covers his eyes. "You sick fuck," he says, grinning. "You're still a two-year-old, Eli."

Eli tries to give Michael Landy the finger, but stumbles and nearly pees on himself, while Mercury squats beside him, urinating a heavy stream.

"Oh yeah, now that's kinda hot."

Mercury succeeds in giving Michael Landy the finger.

"Um—Sheila?"

"*What?*" I look up at Waxed Mustache, knelt over by the camera.

"I think I may have just...turned it off."

I stare at him.

"I was just checking it out for a second, and then the batteries fell out, and now they're all covered with dirt, and—"

An abrupt wave of nausea—I fall to the ground and start to heave.

Rudolf yells from the driver's seat, "I'm outta here in thirty seconds—y'all better get on the bus, or have fun with the poh-leese."

A darkness consumes me, fills up my chest, energy pulsating through my limbs, rising up through my stomach, my throat near-gagging from some invisible mass—like a retching cat coughing up a hairball—and I'm hurling up my insides—acidic, bitter, clumped and tangy—my body merely a vessel designed to release all this accumulated weight.

Moans escape from my system. I rock back and forth on my knees, fluid streaming from all my facial orifices.

"Sheila, come on," Michael Landy grabs my arm and drags me to the bus, my body now sagging behind him, feeling so, so drained—so light now—and so, so tired. I hear the others behind me bickering, shuffling onto the steps, the engine crackling, heating the interior—the bus a terrifying womb abrasively rocking me to sleep.

I dream of a vast snowy landscape in the pitch-blackness of unconsciousness, night. Pointed castles formed of ice and snow border the horizon, towering like massive stalagmites in the foreboding setting. My mother, father, Caleb, and I trek along the icy ashen ground until we approach the entrance of a cave. The cave's entrance is tall, but tight, like the stretching of an open wizard's mouth. A blizzard whirls around us. Ambient bass sounds echo in the backdrop. I know that there is evil here. We climb cautiously into the snow-paved tunnel on some silent, mutually acknowledged mission. I look ahead, trying to spot a reason to retreat, and have a vision of how far the end is, knowing no one else can see. Time shifts and space moves forward rapidly, and we are approaching the end, heaving, shivering, breathing deeply into the night. My mother's way ahead of us, approaching the precipice of the path, descending down into a ruin surrounded by lava. *No, Mom, stop!* Caleb and I are screaming from the top of the precipice. But it's as if she can't even hear us. She continues to walk, slowly down, as if caught in the pull of a witch's spell. My eyes focus on the setting below in the arena-like ruin, where I spot what my mother is walking towards. It's a living copy of herself, gray-skinned and dressed in rags, blood leaking from her head all the way down her body, half of her face torn apart, open and dripping. MOM, we are screaming through the popping lava, PLEASE MOM, COME BACK. But there's no stopping her. She's already gone. She's chosen her own doom.

CALEB

Sheila, r u OK? Tonight in ceremony I felt a huge shift—I was traveling through the depths of space, amongst the most complex of crystalline fractal palaces, consuming vibrant pulsating colors with a clarity I can't even begin to describe... and I burst through this wall of healing Sheils—it was the most beautiful thing I ever felt. I was flying through space at a speed that felt not fast but at this perfect timing with my interior body, this sort of underworld to all the sickness blasting through me like a secret unveiling of the light behind the darkness. It swarmed through my whole body—this light, this TRUTH, working its way into the folds of my organs and bones and right as it almost filled me up right before it burst through my skin is when I saw ur face. I had a vision. It showed me ur soul. Ur frail spirit. It told me that u thought u were going to die. I felt ur spirit's sorrow. I held ur shadow to my chest. I tried to transfer the healing to u—I concentrated so, so hard. I sent u all the love I had. And then I exploded, I lost my body, I lost ur body. Our cells and memories opened up into a swirling galaxy, collapsing into one another, freeing us to the stars!!! I spent a long while spiraling in this bliss, discovering what it means to truly exist. I will have to tell u more in person. These messages can't possibly translate it. But when I came out of it a voice told me that I needed to check in w/u. That u were really in need right now. My flight back to the states isn't for another few weeks, but I want u to know that if u need me, I can leave at a moment's notice. I'm sorry that I was so checked out before. I didn't have any room.

Streaming outside light. Sharp reflection, open window. Brown watermarks on ceiling. Polyester blanket barely covering adjacent collapsed body—nude, facedown. Breathing, yes. My shirt on, jeans on, but unbuttoned, socks on (mostly good signs), location of shoes unknown. Slippery brain. Increased heartbeat. Thirst. A strong scent of frying oil from the street. A toilet upstairs flushing. The aftertaste of bile. A clock on the wall. 7:33 A.M. Skull pounding.

Quietly muster strength to roll off bed. Locate shoes. Take one last look at Michael Landy's squished face, drooling onto pillowcase. Note: this will not happen again.

Dead phone in pocket. Wallet and keys in jacket. Locate front door. Unlock. Escape.

The day enters. Chinatown in the light—a much different experience. The hustle and bustle of restaurants and businesses opening, sizzling pans, beating butcher blocks, shuffling items outdoors for display. The commotion is calmer, gentler, lacking the anxiety that slithers in with the night. I take a deep breath, collect the air deep within my belly and hold it for a moment, before releasing it back to the world.

As I walk through the narrow streets towards the nearest Muni stop, I notice a new lightness—like a tiny pinhole in my brain—releasing the smallest stream of air; an ever-so slight shift in the nature of things. The feeling—like a sort of relief—that the worst is—quite possibly—over. Or, rather, that it couldn't get any worse than this.

The bus pulsates, takes a detour around a closed off street with some outdoor urban market. The doors open. 16th and Mission BART Station, the epicenter of the Mission District's wasteland. I watch through the window. Bodies missing teeth, missing limbs, arched backs, yelling, shouting, smeared with dirt and sweat, urine and feces, a conglomeration of human decay. A city worker in a gas mask sprays a hose into the public restroom. A Mexican woman shouts into a microphone attached to a portable speaker—*Jesus Cristo! Tu salvacion!* She'll stand in this horrific intersection all day, screaming. The pauses in her rough voice where she gasps for air. Wondering, where is this all coming from? This energy, this belief, this drive to engage the outside world through violence.

A riled teenager mounts the rear steps blasting rap music from her smartphone, fills the bus with her disturbed energy, takes a seat in the back with a loud thwack. A small older man wearing a workman's jumpsuit carries a bright orange hard hat to the seat across from me, revealing a gray birthmark that stretches over almost half the right side of his sunburned face. The bus gears up, throbs with movement. I lean against the window, feeling the vibrations charge through my body. The bus stops and releases.

Open doors. External movement.

"Mind if I sit here?"

I glance up at a wobbly, grinning young male carrying a Pink Floyd album and an open container in a brown paper bag.

"It's a free country," I sigh.

He falls into our conjoined seats, sips from the bottle, its label peaking out, *Bulleit Bourbon.* "Check this out—," he thrusts the album in front of me, the iconic prism in dark space. "I found this two blocks up, just lying on the street."

"Cool," I nod.

He shuffles around. "You know, I'm not crazy."

I look at him. "I never said you were."

His eyes are bright hazel, gaping. "I'm not stupid either."

"I'm really not judging you."

"You want some?" He holds out the Bulleit.

I shake my head. "No thanks. It's a little too early for me."

"What time is it?"

"I don't know, my phone's dead. But probably around eight."

"You going to work?"

"No."

"You going home from work?"

"No."

"You're mysterious." He burps. "Ugh, sorry."

The bus halts, honks at a cyclist. The cyclist zooms by. *You must all pay your fair share,* says the robotic recording.

"I had a really long night." He smooths back his shaggy, oily hair.

"Tell me about it."

"I don't really remember much except I've been trying to sit down somewhere for a while. Everywhere I sit, people just keep telling me to move."

"Sorry."

He looks at me with a squinty, boyish smile. "Thanks for listening to me."

"Don't worry about it."

"No, really." His bright eyes become glassy.

I stare at him.

"I'm not crazy, you know." Tears start rolling down his face. The bus halts. The album falls on the floor. He picks it up, sniffling. "I'm not one of those people."

The man with the birthmark is looking at us. A woman laughs loudly on her phone.

"It's okay." My body quietly shakes. I feel this guy's sorrow bleeding into me. He wipes his nose on his sleeve, trying his hardest not to identify with the unsightly manner of his crying. "It's okay." I place my hand on his bony shoulder and he immediately starts bawling. He flings his arms around me. "I'm so sorry," he's sobbing into my neck. "I don't mean to be this way. I really don't." His stink permeates my nostrils as I awkwardly and unwillingly provide support for this weeping stranger, all my senses heightened and telling me DANGER DANGER DAN-GER. I hear the teenager in the back slam her foot on the floor, muttering something angrily; she turns up the volume on her phone. A woman in business dress frowns behind sunglasses. The man with the birthmark stares at me without expression. The beats through the small speaker's static. The body in my arms shakes uncontrollably. I feel his deep sadness in my bones. "It's okay," I whisper to him. "Shh, shh," I close my eyes, rubbing his back in smooth, heavy motions, trying to contain myself. "Don't worry, now. Okay? It's going to be okay."

Inside the apartment, I find Mallory sitting at the kitchen counter in her pajamas with a cup of tea and her iPad. I plug in my phone and fill a French press with coffee grounds that I first spill all over the counter, then use her leftover hot water to pour over it, which only fills it halfway. I plop down on a barstool beside her, groaning.

"You look apocalyptic," she says. A truly fitting description. "I'm worried about you."

"I know, I can feel that from you. And I appreciate it," I say.

"What's the status of the whole project now?"

"Well the deconstruction's complete, but the camera broke, so I think it's pretty much over."

"What are you going to do with the footage?"

"I don't know. Save it, bury it, shoot it up into space?"

"You never know, it might be the most sought after piece in your retrospective one day."

"My retrospective, ha ha."

Mal shrugs, yawning. For the first time since sitting down I notice dark circles under her eyes, a paleness to her skin.

"Are you okay?" I ask.

She sips her tea and places it down, biting her cheeks. "I had a really crazy thing happen to me last night."

The Fifth Wall

"Oh?"

She tells me she was walking home late from work—sometime after midnight—with her keys between her fingers like usual (she'd once had a run-in with an intoxicated man who pushed her up against a wall and knew her name—a customer who once sat at the bar for four hours not ordering anything, muttering comments about her body, whom had to be escorted out by the police—who she'd then kneed in the balls, and, out of fear, ran home before she could report it), and she was walking past a Muni stop, when a timid female voice asked her what time it was. Mal says she stopped, checked the time on her phone, and turned to the woman, who was dressed in layers of ripped clothing and smelled like a dead animal. The woman smiled with jack-o-lantern teeth. "Mallory?" she whispered. And Mallory stared into the woman's eyes, searching for familiarity, while gripping her keys.

"And I realized," she says to me, "It was my *Aunt Millie*." She grasps her forehead. "My Aunt Millie who spent years in and out of halfway houses, who my Irish Catholic grandfather shunned from the family—my parents used to have her over when I was little once in a while for a meal and a shower, but that ended when she tried to pawn my mother's heirloom diamond earrings—anyway, I was like, *Oh my God, you remember me after all these years?* And she just nodded. I asked her if she was okay, and she said yes. She asked how my parents were, and I gave her the basics, and then we just stood there for what felt like a half an hour, just looking at each other, her hands cupped on my cheeks, smiling with this pure *joy*. When I got home I started bawling."

"Wow," I stare at her. "Did you know she was still alive?"

Mallory shakes her head. "This city, I tell you—it's so easy to lose yourself in, but you always turn up somewhere."

You might have the concern that you're walking back in the same direction that you came from, but you're not.

173

"What does the Oracle have to say about it?" I ask.

She smiles, reaching in her pajama pocket for her phone. "I actually got a really good one earlier this morning."

I lean over her shoulder as she reads the text out loud. *"What is needed is OBLIVION. This is a time for either total despair, or madness. Create, create, die, and repeat. Then set this language on fire."*

"The Oracle's becoming meta," I say.

Mallory nods, laughing, clutching the phone to her heart in a gesture of deep gratitude.

Outside, the sound of a child falling. The consoling murmur of a teacher. The sounds of walking canes.

"And what about you?" Mallory says. "Weren't you going to a lecture?"

It's about looking at the whole—the here and the void simultaneously. It's a different way of remembering.

I look at her, knowing that I have to tell my brother about our house. And perhaps my dad, at some point. They both deserve to know.

The counter vibrates. My phone returning to life. Suspended messages now recovering, like traces of the dead. The uncertainty and unknowns of Adam possibly only an app away. But, oddly, I find myself disinterested. Adam and I ended that night in the desert; we'd just both been too weak to admit it.

"Oh—by the way," Mal reaches over to a side drawer in the cabinet adjacent to the bar. "That hot contractor came by the other day and dropped off something for you."

"Jesse?"

"Yeah, that sounds about right. Little frame, big muscles, a bit *too* friendly."

"That's Jesse."

"I was in a rush out the door, and it looked kind of dirty so I just tossed it in this drawer, and kept forgetting about it."

"What is it?"

The Fifth Wall

She hands me a plastic bag wrapped around a hard, heavy mass. I open the bag and the object is caked in soil. It looks like a metal canister of some sort.

"He said one of his 'guys' found it while digging up one of the shrubberies. He thought you might want it."

Confused, I look more closely at the object.

"Holy fuck," I say.

"What?"

"It's the time capsule—the one from the video."

Mal leans over, inspects the contents of the bag. "Well shit."

I stare silently at the sooty object for a few moments, trying to imagine what my mother might have put in it. The video only showed a glimpse of her cutting strips of white paper. What could she have possibly been making? Miniature origami? Some bizarre, blank collage? A fear enters—that whatever's inside the box won't be good enough. No physical object could possibly sustain the importance of what should be inside of it—could make any part of what's happened okay.

"Are we waiting for some sort of audience?" Mallory holds up her hands.

I shut the bag, wrap it tightly around the time capsule, and place it on the counter.

"I'm not ready to look at it," I say.

There are coincidences, and then there are consequences. We attract the realities around us by our actions, with our energies and intentions.

The show is happening all around us.

We write our own dialogues, record our own voiceovers. We act from bodies with minds we think of as ours, on staged sets we call reality, until a glitch happens, and we lose control.

But did we ever really have it in the first place?

I enrolled in a graduate art program to continue a journey of intellectualizing the world—what I'd always considered a raw talent, but now think of as a flaw I was infected with in the womb. A lack of agency, of will, encoded like a glitch in my rebellious organism.

How to make a life for one's self now, knowing of the presence of this deep dragon deep within me, awoken permanently from its slumber, breathing fire onto everything I thought I knew?

I'm not sure that I can go back.

In a few days I'll receive an email containing the data translation of my body in organized charts of letters and numbers. The full decryption of my living system; a scientific Oracle handing me my future. I'll read between the lines for patterns and signs, some indication—some clue to the secrets of my chemistry, of this *Lack* that permeates my existence—the constant feeling that I'm missing something just beneath the surface—that if I remembered just one more detail, I'd wake up from a great fog of amnesia—a theatrical light falling from an empty blue

The Fifth Wall

sky, the glimpse of a white rabbit in the corner of my eye—I'd remember what everything around me has been training me to forget.

I'll finally understand. This body will speak.

It's the hero who always speaks the last word before dying, I hear my father in my head quoting Barthes. But there are no heroes anymore. All we have are recordings.

The film furrows and chafes. Black and white lines zigzag on the color image. My mother looks directly at the camera. Her face becomes large and bright, like the sun. Her lips curve up to the left. My dad asks her a question, and she answers it. Both voices are deep, growling hums—robotic, unearthly, alien—the tape's own language of absence, signals piercing through the noise, waning with each play. My mother looks directly at the camera, as if she's looking right at me—a face that holds such power over any memory, her ghostly image coordinates drifting in the horizontal streaks, soon to be lost to the static.

So beautiful in all their terror.

Acknowledgments

I am deeply indebted to Stephen Beachy for his dedicated time, interest and guidance at all various stages of this book. His intellectual generosity and spirited intuition were (and continue to be) simply invaluable. I also deeply thank The Lighthouse Works Fellowship for providing me six weeks on an island of winter bliss with an incomparable artist community, during which I rewrote nearly two thirds of the final draft.

Thanks so much to my agent, Priscilla Reagan, for her hard work and relentless cheer and humor (and to Bill Creighton for our introduction). And many thanks to my editor at Black Sparrow Books, Chelsea Bingham, for her strong support and belief in my work.

Thank you to Lewis Buzbee and Nina Schuyler for their direction and encouragement during the early stages of this book, and to my fiction writing workshops at the University of San Francisco for their instrumental feedback and discussions.

I am particularly grateful to Anthony Baab for our many conversations about contemporary art, not to mention the most stunning book cover. And to Courtney Moreno, Tiffany Wong, Audrey Baker, Michael Rebinski, Michael R. Jacobs, Gray Tolhurst, Ariella Robinson, Bradley Fest, Bill Stubler and Christine Hellberg for their consistent interest, insights and ears. And a special thanks to Robert Lee Haycock for his expert art museum knowledge, and also to Chuck Kinder for his continuous good humor, encouragement and support. Moreover, thank you to countless other friends and family who have supported and inspired me along the way.

A heartfelt and endlessly expansive thanks to Daniel Martin for his constant care, wisdom and support during much of the process of writing this book; without his involvement in my life, I honestly don't know where or how I would be today.

And lastly, thank you from the bottom of my heart to Michaelangelo—his endless love, support, intellect, wisdom and magic have been quite frankly the portal to my wildest dreams.

RACHEL NAGELBERG is an American novelist, poet, and conceptual artist living in Los Angeles. *The Fifth Wall* is her debut novel.